THREE THINGS I'D NEVER DO

REMI CARRINGTON

Copyright ©2020 Pamela Humphrey
All Rights Reserved
Phrey Press
www.phreypress.com
www.remicarrington.com
First Edition

This is a work of fiction. Names, characters, businesses, places, events, and incidents are either the products of the author's imagination or used in a fictitious manner. Any resemblance to actual persons, living or dead, or actual events is purely coincidental.

All rights reserved. This book or any portion thereof may not be reproduced or used in any manner whatsoever without the express written permission of the publisher except for the use of brief quotations in a book review.

Photo credit: Mimagephotos, DepositPhotos.com
ISBN-13: 978-1-947685-28-4

❊ Created with Vellum

CHAPTER 1

There were three things I said I'd never do—move back in with my parents, let my mother set me up, and date a guy with a dog. But thanks to an unexpected bolt of lightning and my mom's persistence, I'd already scratched two of those off my list. Technically, the second one I'd only agreed to. I hadn't actually gone on the blind date. *Yet*. That special type of fun was scheduled for tomorrow night.

I could hardly contain my excitement.

It had been a long summer, and this was only the first week of July.

When my cute, little, all-to-myself three-bedroom house was struck by lightning in late May, I was forced to move back home. But only temporarily.

My sanity clung to that one word. Temporarily.

Understandably, I was eager for the repairs on my house to be finished. But expecting contractors to finish on schedule only set me up for disappointment. That didn't stop me from going to the house just to check on the progress.

Because of the pickup parked at an angle in my driveway, I had to park on the street, which gave me time to admire my house as I went to the door. Repairs to the outside made it impossible to tell lightning had targeted my house. "Hello?" The place seemed eerily quiet.

Derek, my ever-helpful contractor, hadn't texted back when I mentioned stopping by, but I showed up anyway.

"Eve?" He poked his head around the corner. "I didn't know you were coming today." His chipper greeting worried me. Derek was rarely chipper.

"I sent you a message."

"The repairs are coming along." That was code for 'they aren't done yet.'

I stepped past him, flashing my sweetest smile. "Oh, I know. I just wanted to take a peek. I'll stay out of the way." I headed for the master bedroom, the part of the house still being fixed.

If the water hadn't been turned off during the repairs, I'd have moved into the guest room and put up with contractors and workers traipsing through my space. But I couldn't figure out how to live without water.

Derek stayed close. "The flooring didn't come in yesterday as expected. But it should be here Monday."

It wasn't the end of the world, but it meant more time. "How long will it take to install?"

"A few days. Maybe a week." He hooked a thumb toward the master bath. "The painter messed up. That's what I get for hiring my brother-in-law."

Bracing for the worst, I ran to the bathroom. "Ugh. The fifties called. They want their bathroom back. Bubblegum pink? It was supposed to be a soothing aqua."

Derek ran his fingers through his grey hair. "I'm leaving to buy the right color soon. Painting won't take long. Then we just have the flooring and the baseboards."

"One more week?" Surviving at my parents' house was a struggle few understood.

"Probably." Derek was the king of non-committal.

Purse on my shoulder, I walked outside before I ranted or cried. Neither would help the situation. "Call me when it's ready." I glanced up at the canopy of my massive oak tree. I missed my house.

"I will. And don't worry. I fired the painter. I'll be sleeping on the couch for a week, but I can't do much about that."

"Sorry." I felt a little bad for Derek, but I did for me too. I'd taken off the afternoon for nothing.

I sat in the Volkswagen, staring at the house. I just wanted my life to settle back into normal. Before pulling away from the curb, I clicked the name at the top of my favorites. Talking to my best friend always brightened my day. "Hey. I went by the house today."

"And?" Haley had heard all about my house troubles.

"There is no longer a hole in the front of my house, but the flooring was delayed, and they painted the bathroom an awful shade of pink. Besides all that, it looks great."

"Sorry. How much longer?"

"A week maybe. But I'm not sure I'll survive another week at my parents' house. I've put on ten pounds in two months. Mom offers me every sweet thing imaginable then lectures about how I should take better care of myself so I can attract a man."

"My couch is yours whenever you want it."

I wasn't quite ready to give up a queen-size bed for a couch. "Don't be surprised if I show up this week. Want to grab dinner later?"

"Sure. What time do you get off work?"

"I took the afternoon off. I think I'm going to take a calming bubble bath, then I'll call you."

"You still going out tomorrow?" The laughter following her question did not go unnoticed.

"Don't remind me. Mom won't tell me the guy's name or anything about him except that he's *muy guapo*."

"How are you supposed to know who you're meeting?"

"I'm supposed to walk into the restaurant carrying a yellow rose." It sounded so much worse when I said the words out loud.

When Haley finally caught her breath, she cleared her throat. "Seriously? A yellow rose?"

"We are in Texas after all. I'm sure my mom thought it was a wonderful idea." "The Yellow Rose of Texas" would probably be stuck on repeat in my head the rest of the day.

Haley laughed all over again. "I still can't believe you let your mom set you up."

"She wore me down. I got tired of telling her no."

"Eve, it's called threatening."

"Yeah, well, to Mom that's just adding motivation. But it's only one date. How bad can it be?"

"Bad enough that you'll wish you never asked that question. Eek. I gotta go. Dinner sounds good. Call me later." When it came to friends, Haley was the best of the best.

The drive to my parents' house didn't take long. Traffic hadn't spooled up yet, and I lived just far enough away that it was inconvenient if they drove over and found no one home but close enough that they'd never need to spend the night. At least that was part of my rationale for buying in that area.

It wasn't where I'd grown up. After all the kids had left the house, Mom and Dad moved out of their small town and bought a house in the city thirty minutes down the road. I loved San Antonio, but I sometimes missed Stadtburg. Living there was its own kind of interesting.

Tonight would give me a reprieve. My parents were gone for the night, and their quick trip to see their only grandbaby meant I would get to enjoy a quiet house. Out of habit, I parked along the curb and was out of the car before I thought about it. Moving my VW was too much trouble.

I breathed in the smell of fresh-cut grass. For early July, the weather was surprisingly pleasant. That wasn't always the case in San Antonio.

I waved at the neighbor, slightly alarmed at the chainsaw in his hand. What did an eighty-five-year-old man need with a chainsaw? He had kids and grandkids who were better suited for that type—any type—of work.

"Evening, Mr. Raymond."

"Hello, Eve."

"What are you doing with that? It looks dangerous." I stopped long enough to hear his response.

Mr. Raymond snickered. "*Dangerous*. You sound like my wife. But you sure don't look like her." The man was losing his filter. "I'm going to trim my tree a little. Not hard at all." He set the chainsaw on the ground and leaned a ladder against the tree.

Combining ladders and chainsaws seemed even more dangerous than either one by itself, but why bother saying anything? He had no interest in listening to me or his wife.

"Be careful." That seemed the polite thing to say.

My keys jingled as I dropped them on the entry table, and my purse landed on top of them. "Pookie, I'm home."

Enjoying freedom, my fuzzy black kitten ran up the hall then slipped on the tile as she tried to stop.

When my parents were home, the poor kitten had to be confined to my room. What kind of people didn't like cats? I gave her a good scratch as I carried her to the bedroom. "I'll fill your food bowl and get you fresh water, then I'm going to take a bath. Please stay out of trouble while I do."

She didn't answer, which probably meant she was ignoring my every word. As soon as food landed in her bowl, she ate, and I turned on the hot water.

My room wasn't fancy, but it was comfortable. The bed was draped with a pink comforter—my mom's favorite color. It was a nicer bed than I'd had growing up. But the same long dresser I'd had in my room all through high school sat against the wall. Some drawers had memories stuffed in them—things of mine that Mom wanted me to keep. The others were empty, but I didn't use them.

While the tub filled, I slipped out of my shirt and laid it over my suitcase—not putting stuff in drawers made the stay seem less temporary. Temporary was the word I used to console myself when my parents acted like I was a teen again.

My other clothes were tossed all over the bed and floor, but cleaning that could wait until after I'd had time to relax in the tub. I wasn't the neatest person in the world, but no one complained . . . except my mother.

I walked into the bathroom, and if not for the overflow drain, water might have spilled over the edge. I needed to drain off a little or the floor would be covered in puddles when I slid my not-so-skinny body into the water. While the water drained, I slipped out of my jeans, ran back to the bedroom, and laid them beside my shirt, hoping Pookie wouldn't nap on them.

With my hair pinned up in a messy twist and my phone—positioned far away from the tub—playing my favorite playlist, I slid under the bubbles.

The entire bathroom was painted a bright yellow. I'd never liked that color when I was younger, and I liked it even less now. Yellow was my least favorite color. It didn't give me a warm and sunny feeling. I'd choose any variation of blue every day of the week, but even gray or beige were better than yellow.

Of course Mom would choose that color for the rose I

had to take on the date. It wasn't even worth countering with a different idea.

I closed my eyes, as the warmth and bubbles almost made me forget my problems. Almost.

Mr. Raymond and his chainsaw could barely be heard over the music.

Humming along, I sank into the tub. There were few pleasures that compared to a hot bubble bath.

An eerie creaking sound made me wonder what Pookie was into. Was it worth getting out of the tub? Whatever mess she'd made, I could clean up later. I didn't even bother opening my eyes.

A loud crash shook the house, something clawed at my face, and a sharp pain radiated through my leg. Now I didn't want to open my eyes.

Pookie was much too small to cause such havoc.

As I pushed up out of the water, my head hit something hard and large. Why was there a tree branch as wide as my hips in the bathroom? My gut said it had something to do with Mr. Raymond and that stupid chainsaw.

The branches were too dense to push through. With the tree across the tub and the way the big branches were situated, I couldn't get out. If I'd been sitting up or even standing beside the tub, I'd be in a world of hurt ... or dead.

How much of the house was damaged? I couldn't see enough to know how the rest of the bathroom looked, but considering there was a tree in the bathroom, it couldn't be good.

Bits of sunshine cut through the dense canopy of leaves.

I couldn't let myself think about how bad things were or about how I could've died. Right now, I was alive, but I needed to get out of the tub.

No helpful ideas popped into my head.

Forcing myself to breathe in and out slowly, I focused on keeping my face out of the water.

Sirens sounded in the distance.

My phone had survived because George Strait was still singing "The Fireman."

Connecting those two things, I questioned whether I'd survive the ordeal. The tree hadn't killed me, but embarrassment might.

Using my toes, I worked to let only a little water out. I needed the bubbles to keep me covered, but I also liked breathing air.

Voices echoed in the house. I hoped it was someone to rescue me and not Mr. Raymond.

"I'm in here! In the bathroom."

Footsteps pounded up the hall. "Hello?"

"I'm stuck in the tub." I hollered out that tidbit so whoever it was could at least be prepared to find me covered only in bubbles.

I wasn't prepared. Hopefully the bubbles lasted a while.

A fireman poked his head through the door. Well, from my vantage point it was a shadow with a voice, which I assumed belonged to a fireman. "You in here?"

"Yes, in the tub."

Leaves rustled. "Are you hurt?"

"I don't think so, but the tree has me barricaded in here."

"Were you injured when it fell?"

I'd already said I wasn't hurt. Why was he asking if I was injured?

That reinforced my thoughts from earlier. The damage must've been severe, and he was surprised to find someone alive.

I mentally took inventory. I'd been too panicked to think about what parts of me were in pain. "I don't know. My leg hurts a bit, but the water hasn't turned red."

His radio squawked. "Female in the tub. Bathroom at the end of the hall." Leaves rustled again. He must've been pushing his way into the room. "My name is Adam. We'll get you out of here. What's your name?"

"Evelyn Taylor, but everyone calls me Eve." At that moment, I wished my parents had named me Sue or Paula, anything other than Eve.

He had the courtesy not to ask if I was pulling his leg. "How old are you, Eve?"

"Twenty-nine. Really. There's no again."

He chuckled, which meant he'd caught my humor. "Was there anyone else in the house?"

The question sparked horror.

"Pookie! Where's Pookie?"

The cat had never been outside. She wouldn't know what to do. She might run off. I blinked, trying not to cry. Or had she been crushed?

"Pookie?" The helpful fireman kept his voice calm. "Is that a dog?"

The main thing the tree wiped out—other than the house and my dignity—was my filter. With my mind racing and my mouth spewing, words didn't slow long enough to run through a filter. "I would *never* own a dog. Pookie is a kitten, a poor helpless kitten. She's black and fuzzy."

Adam gave sort of a grunt, which made me think he didn't care for cats. "Once we get you to safety, I'll see about finding Pookie. I'll need to cut away the branches so we can get you out, but we don't want this big branch to shift."

"You mean fall on me."

"We don't want that. I'm going to get some tools in here and cut away a few of these branches so you can get out of that tub." The radio squawked again. "I have a twenty-nine-year-old female trapped in the bathtub by the downed tree. She says that, besides a kitten, she was the only one home."

He'd mentioned my kitten, which elevated him to something just below superhero status. If he got me out of the tub in time for dinner without me dying of embarrassment, he might hit superhero before the night was over.

"Can you tell me what day it is?"

"Friday. It's Friday. I was planning to go to dinner with my friend. Do you think I'll still be able to go out later?" Why was I asking him stupid questions? For that matter, why was he asking stupid questions?

"We'll do our best to make that happen. Can you tell me who the president is?"

If Haley had asked the question, there were multiple ways I could answer, but I didn't know this guy, and he was only trying to assess how badly I'd been thumped on the head. "The tree didn't hit me that hard."

He chuckled. "What year is it?"

"The same year it was yesterday. I hope. Because if that tree was some type of portal and you're a robot, I'm not going to survive this." I desperately wanted to see who was talking to me. My hope was that it wasn't a young, handsome firefighter.

Was that hope rational? No.

Was it stupid? Yes.

Did either of those truths change my wish? Nope.

Waiting to be rescued made me antsy, but asking him about my cat every two seconds wouldn't help get me out any faster, so I kept my worry to myself. I couldn't take much more of the branches in my face, so I worked my hand up through the smaller limbs and tried to push them away.

The bigger branch shifted, and the little bit of pain in my leg exploded into a lot of pain. I yelped.

"You okay, Eve? Where does it hurt?" His voice stayed even. He could've given lessons in calm, not that I was in any frame of mind to learn anything right then.

"My leg." I slid my hand to where it hurt. "I have a gash, it feels like. And one of the smaller branches is jabbing in that spot."

"I'm going to reach in and break off that part that's poking you. I need you to stay still and guide my hand."

"Yeah, well, every time I move, more bubbles pop, which is concerning. And I can't see your hand."

Fingers brushed mine. "Tell me about Pookie. Where did you get him?" My rescuer was just an outline on the other side of the leaves, one with a deep, smooth voice. And he had a massive, calloused hand.

Why was I thinking about his hand, the one that just brushed against my thigh? And why hadn't I shaved my legs? Of course this would happen at the beginning of my bath.

The voice didn't sound like it belonged to an old guy, one with a herd of grandchildren. I didn't know why I cared. But the idea of a young, good-looking fireman standing on the other side of those leaves tied my stomach in knots.

Curiosity ate at me. I really wanted to know what he looked like. "Pookie is a girl. She was a rescue. Someone left her in a box at a pet store. I've had her since she was about eight weeks old."

"It sounds like she's a lucky girl."

The offending twig snapped, and the pain in my leg eased. "You got it. Thanks."

"Now I just have to get rid of these big ones. Or at least one of them."

My nerves got the better of me, and I started to ramble. "This is my parents' house. I don't live here. I'm only staying here while *my* house gets repaired. It was hit by lightning in that big storm. While I'm living here, my kitty has to stay in the bedroom unless my parents aren't home. And they are gone for the weekend, so that's why she wasn't locked up in my room. But she's so far from home. If she gets out and I lose her, I don't know what I'll do."

"Why don't you try calling her?" His outline moved away for a minute.

"Good idea. I can do that." I sucked in a deep breath. "Pookie. Here, kitty kitty." My voice shook a bit. Crying would make me seem weak and fragile. I didn't want that.

The outline reappeared, and leaves rustled. Fingers poked through the branches. "Can you reach my hand? If you can, squeeze it for me, Eve."

I slipped my hand out of the water and grabbed his fingers.

His hand was warm.

I needed to stop thinking about his hands. "Please hurry. The bubbles are popping, and that's all that's keeping me covered. Well, that and the leaves, but you're about to cut those away. If I grab a few and position them correctly, maybe I'll look like Eve in the Sunday school pictures."

His chuckle only spurred me on.

"But really, my hair isn't long enough for that. And it's up. If I'd known I would need it as a covering, I would've left it down. But in the pictures in Sunday school, Eve was always standing behind really big leaves. These leaves are little. Isn't it funny to have such a big tree with so many tiny leaves?" Why did my mouth keep moving?

"I can't say I've ever really thought about it."

"When I get nervous, I ramble. I'm sorry."

"No need to apologize."

"Walking out of here will be interesting. And by interesting, I mean horribly embarrassing. Was Mr. Raymond hurt?" My thoughts jumped around like bingo balls in a spinner. And every one of those thoughts flew right out of my mouth. Surprisingly, I hadn't asked him how old he was.

"If by Mr. Raymond you mean the older gentleman who

managed to accidentally down half of a two-hundred-year-old tree. I saw him outside as I walked in. He looked unharmed. His wife seemed to be pretty angry though. Hang on a sec." The radio made a noise. "Harper, balled up in my seat is one of the charity t-shirts. Will you bring it to me?"

"Be there in two shakes, Cardona."

Cardona? Hearing the last name had my brain conjuring images. "Do you have to rescue people from downed trees often?"

"We had quite a few trees go down during that big storm. I'm guessing it was the same one that damaged your house. We do some rescues, but not all people are quite as lucky as you." The branches moved a little as the chainsaw ground against the bark.

Keeping quiet while he worked was hard. But as soon as the noise died down, I was at it again. "I thought about that. If I'd been standing up, it would have been bad."

"But you weren't, so we'll focus on that. What do you do for a living?"

"I work in IT." I didn't bother to get into the specifics of what I did because most people didn't understand it anyway.

"Do you like it?" The saw continued to idle, making conversation possible.

"Well enough." I shivered, making everything shake.

"If you're cold and if you can reach the drain, let the water out. I have a guy bringing in a shirt. And it might be good for your leg not to be in the water."

"A shirt? That's great, but you realize that I was *completely* without clothes in the bath. Not just without a shirt."

He stifled a snicker. "I understand. But I'm working with what I've got. If I can save you from the tree, I'll also do my best to save you from embarrassment."

"What do you mean *if* you can save me from the tree?"

"I didn't mean if. *When*. When I save you."

Maybe I could channel my rambling into something a bit more conversational and less random. "How long have you been a fireman?"

"Seven years." He wasn't an old guy. Dang it.

The engine revved again, and the big branch vibrated as he worked. Since there wasn't much else to do, when he paused the motor, I took that opportunity to see if Pookie was within earshot. "Pookie!"

Leaves rustled. A branch snapped.

"Ow!" Adam no longer sounded calm.

"Did you hurt yourself? Are you okay?" I had visions of his arm dangling by a tendon. I tried shifting the branches.

"I found Pookie." His voice sounded tense. "Stay still, please."

"Are you talking to me or Pookie?"

"*You* need to stay still." He muttered a word that would've gotten my mouth washed out with soap as a kid.

"Is she alive?"

"And scratching. She'd climbed up into the tree apparently, and then jumped down onto my back when you called her."

"Sorry." I kicked at the drain. "Do you need me to hold her?" Holding a kitten in a bathtub when I had no layers of protection ranked as my worst idea ever.

"No. I'll have one of the guys keep her wrangled for now." He moved back toward the door. "Here, Harper, keep Pookie safe. She has all her claws."

"Will do. Hey there, fuzzball. Aren't you a cutie? Did the big tree scare you?" Harper's soothing conversation with the cat faded.

Harper seemed to like cats. Maybe he was young and unattached. Why did I care? Seeing any of these guys again would send me running. I'd never want to see them again, let alone date any of them.

"Let me know when the water has drained, and I'll hand in the shirt." Adam shifted the largest tree limb, but only a little. "I'm going to move the big one away from your head. Then if you can stand, we'll get you out of here."

I moved the leaves aside far enough to get a better look and finally caught sight of Adam. Of course, he was looking down, and my gaze connected with the most amazing brown eyes. Gold flecks were sprinkled in the soft brown surrounding the dark brown center. After more than a second—it felt more like ten minutes—I noticed the rest of his face.

Why did they have to send this guy to rescue me? He was calendar material. My embarrassment multiplied exponentially.

I stuck out my hand. "I'm ready for the shirt."

He handed in a navy-blue t-shirt, still wadded. "Once I move this and you get up, I'll need to check for injuries. But if you get that on, I'll find you something else to cover . . . other parts."

Other parts. How charming. Haley was never going to believe any of this. Did I even want to tell her?

"What are the other guys doing? It seems to me like you're the one doing all the work."

"They are making sure the house doesn't fall down on top of us." Inch by inch, the downed limb moved away from my head.

There had to be significant muscle in those arms to move that tree. But that probably wasn't what I needed to focus on.

All the shifting knocked a towel off the shelf on the wall. Either that or God dropped it straight down from heaven. Giving me his back, Adam held out the bright yellow towel. It matched the walls perfectly.

"Can you stand? How's your leg?" He turned as if he were going to look over his shoulder.

"Don't look. Give me a sec." Grabbing onto the sides of the tub, I wriggled myself into a standing position. I didn't have the ability—or the agility—to spring up without effort. Finally upright, I pulled the navy shirt over my head and wrapped the towel around the parts the shirt didn't cover.

My mom hadn't pitched for big, luxurious towels. This one was slightly larger than a hand towel. The corners connected at my hip, but the big gap showed off my leg . . . all the way up.

I didn't bother answering the unimportant questions. "I've got the shirt on, and the towel is strategically placed. What do you need to check?"

He turned, and his gaze swept over me. Checking me out now held a whole new meaning. "Only thing that hurts is your leg?" He shoved branches aside and stepped closer.

I managed a quick nod.

He lifted the edge of the towel, but only a little. Why hadn't I positioned the gap on the side that was injured?

"The medic will need to take a look at that." His gaze shifted to my face, and he brushed his thumb along my cheek.

I might've gasped without meaning to.

He yanked his hand away. "Sorry. Do the scratches sting?"

"There are scratches on my face?" Smooth, that was me.

He pretended like I hadn't just embarrassed myself. "A few. They don't look deep. But you need to have that leg looked at." His gaze dropped to the gap, and he shrugged off his fireman coat. "Put this on. Then we'll head outside."

The coat was significantly longer than his shirt. Thankfully.

He'd officially hit superhero status.

CHAPTER 2

Standing near the ambulance, I tried not to be obvious as I scanned for one more glimpse of Adam. I knew full well my attraction—that was too strong a word, my interest—was driven by adrenaline and the fact that he'd just saved me and my kitten.

Pookie? Where did they have her stashed?

Several firemen walked out of the house and gathered in the yard. Which one was Harper? I could ask him about where he'd put Pookie.

"Hold still, miss." The nice paramedic lady cleaned the gash on my leg and covered it with gauze. "You probably need a few stitches. Would you like us to transport you to the hospital?"

No part of me wanted to go to a hospital. "No, I'll have my friend come get me, and we'll find an urgent care."

"All right. Will you please sign this then?" She held out a clipboard.

Calling my friend would be complicated by the fact that my phone was buried under insulation and tree branches in the bathroom, but I'd figure something out.

When Haley and I joked about guys, there was never anything above superhero. That was the top tier. We'd never needed to think of anything above that. But when Adam showed up next to me, holding my suitcase in one hand and a kitty carrier in the other, I knew then that dinner would be centered on identifying a new tier.

He glanced back at the house. "They don't want anyone going inside right now."

Anyone meant me.

"But I figured you'd need clothes. I guessed that the bedroom closest to the bathroom was yours and gathered up as much as I could off the bed and the floor." He lifted the carrier. "This sitting next to the bed was another hint I had the right room. And here's Pookie."

Crap! Now he was cleaning up after me. How much more embarrassing could this day get?

I smiled and prayed that I wouldn't tear up. "Thank you so much. Let me run next door and put clothes on, then I'll give you the coat back." With suitcase in hand, I turned toward the Raymond's house. "You can put Pookie next to my car. I just need . . ." Every time one problem was solved, another was discovered.

"Where are your keys?"

"Next to my purse on the table just inside the front door. Do you think they'd let me just reach in and grab it?" I tugged at the bottom hem of the coat. It grew shorter as my nerves ramped up.

"You go change. I'll get the keys." He stopped and turned, reaching into his pocket. "Here's your phone."

That explained why I could hear Johnny Cash singing "Flushed from the Bathroom of Your Heart." My phone was mocking me. The whole world was mocking me.

"Thanks." I wanted to tuck the phone in a pocket, but that coat had so many, I was afraid I'd lose it.

Adam headed back toward the house like he was on a mission.

Mrs. Raymond ushered me into her house as soon as I stepped onto her porch. "I am so sorry. Please apologize to your parents for me."

My parents. I needed to tell them. If I timed it all just right, I could be at dinner with Haley when they made it back to town. Having Mom fuss over me was not the way I wanted to spend the evening.

With the gash on my leg, leggings caused me pain, so I pulled on a pair of shorts. And I put on a bra, but I kept his t-shirt on. It smelled like cologne, not one of those strong, offensive ones either. I stopped sniffing the shirt long enough to close my suitcase.

I seriously needed to stop thinking about the good-looking firefighter with the great-smelling shirt and the warm, massive hands.

Easier said than done.

Adam was waiting near my car. "Your keys and purse."

"I don't know what to say." Embarrassed and grateful, I wasn't sure whether to throw my arms around his neck or back away slowly.

His gaze dropped to my leg, which set off a riot of butterflies inside me. "You should really get that looked at."

He was starting to slip off that top tier. Telling me what I should do was the quickest way to irritate me.

"I will. I need to call a friend and let my parents know that their house has a hole in the roof and wall. How bad is the damage? Is the whole back of the house just gone?"

From the front, the only clue that something bad had happened was the leaning tree that disappeared into the house. The back of the house probably looked horrible.

He crinkled his nose and nodded. "The bathroom was the worst of it, but the damage is significant."

"Thanks for saving me."

He nodded but didn't leave. Was he waiting for something? Working up the nerve to say something? Or ask something? My brain latched onto that thought like a new golden trinket.

I swallowed and looked at the ground.

After a few uncomfortable seconds, he cleared his throat.

My gaze snapped up to meet his.

He pointed at the coat in my arms. "I need that back."

"Oh! Of course." I handed it over, feeling like a special kind of stupid. "And I'll run back and change out of this shirt."

"You can keep my shirt."

"Thanks." Tempted to hug him but determined not to embarrass myself further, I marched away—well it probably looked more like a limp or a hobble because my leg was starting to throb in the worst way. I called Haley. "Hi. I cannot explain it all right now, but I need you to come get me. And I'll need to borrow your couch tonight."

"That changed quickly. What happened?"

"A tree fell on the house. Please hurry." I kept my back to the commotion behind me. If the handsome firefighter was looking this way, I didn't want to know.

"A what what? Oh my gosh. I'm grabbing my keys right now. Be there soon." She ended the call then called right back. "Are you okay?"

"I just have a gash on my leg. I probably need stitches." But no, I really wasn't okay. I needed to get far away from this place and these people.

"On my way."

I set Pookie's carrier in the backseat and tossed the suitcase beside it. After multiple deep breaths, I made the second call. "Mom, hi. I have some bad news."

"You cannot change your mind about tomorrow night. If

you cancel, you will be hosting Thanksgiving and Christmas at your house, and you'll be the one to cook." Mom could be quite convincing.

"I'm not canceling. Y'all should come home. Mr. Raymond was trimming his trees, and—"

"Ay that man. Did he hurt himself?"

"He accidently cut down part of his big tree, and it fell on the house—your house."

The longest stretch of silence I'd ever heard from my mom—excluding the times when she was furious with me—played out over the phone.

"Mom?"

"The whole house?"

My mind raced to remember how Adam had worded it. "The back bathroom got the worst of it, but the damage is significant."

Mom hollered at dad, not bothering to cover the mouthpiece or even pull the phone away.

When she finished explaining, I jumped back into the conversation. "Haley is picking me up, so I won't be here when you get back. But I'm okay." I waffled on whether or not to mention my minor injury or the whole bathtub part.

"Just stay there. You can keep looters out until we get home."

I was in no mood to battle looters. "My leg is hurt, and I need to see a doctor."

"Injured? Mr. Raymond will be getting a lecture. He almost got my little girl killed."

"It's a gash on the leg, Mom. I'll live." I wasn't going to tell her how right she was. "Besides, I think Mrs. Raymond has taken care of the lecture part."

"She better take away that chainsaw."

"Agreed. I'll call you later." My leg continued to throb, and I scanned the street, hoping Haley would hurry.

As I waited in the car, my nerves settled. The firemen walked in and out of the house, but when my dark-haired, good-looking rescuer glanced toward my car, my interest or attraction—or whatever it was—morphed into complete embarrassment.

If I never saw Adam Cardona again, it would be too soon.

∽

Sprawled on Haley's couch, I stroked Pookie as my fuzzball purred. Cats could be very therapeutic.

"He picked up your clothes and put them in the suitcase?" Haley swiped at fruit on her phone screen.

"That was like number three on the list of embarrassing things today." I shifted, trying to decide if taking something for the pain was worth the effort of getting up.

"Please tell me your cute undergarments were packed."

"I'm trying *not* to think about what he touched and what was packed. It's bad enough that my stuff was strewn all over the floor. The sooner I put this ordeal behind me, the better I'll feel."

"He reached superhero status, huh?"

"Yeah. Even after my cat scratched him, he kept her safe." I scratched Pookie behind the ears. "But you were scared. You didn't mean to hurt the nice fireman, did you?"

"You going to see him again?"

"Hopefully not. If I ran into him at a grocery store, I'd turn around and walk the other way. The full embarrassment has settled in. My mind blocked it out somewhat when it was happening, but I was in the tub *without clothes on*. I don't know how much he could see through the leaves."

"Gummy worms or ice cream?" Haley pushed up off the floor. Like my mother, to Haley, food was love.

"Both, but only if you have vanilla."

"With a name like Adam, I think he's perfect for you!" Haley dodged the pillow I tossed her way, laughing. "Dessert will be out in a minute. How's your leg?"

"It hurts. I can't believe I needed stitches."

"I'll bring you something for the pain." Haley disappeared around the corner.

My phone rang. If I didn't answer Mom's call, she'd be at the door in under ten minutes.

I took a deep breath and swiped at the screen. "Hi, Mom. Did y'all make it back into town?"

"We—" Sobs drowned out the rest of her words.

I waited. Her reaction wasn't entirely unexpected.

"Hey, sweetheart." Dad's voice was considerably calmer.

"Hi, Dad."

"We're glad you're all right. Mom is imagining the many ways it could have turned out differently."

"Even my cat is fine. Tell her not to cry. But I am sorry about the house."

"It'll turn out okay. Do you need me to get you a hotel?"

"I'm fine at Haley's." Hearing my mom sob in the background, I tried not to cry. "And tell Mom that I'll still be able to go tomorrow night." I offered that as a glimmer of hope, something for her to look forward to. Deep down, I didn't want to go.

Would makeup cover the scratches on my face?

Did it matter? I'd promised Mom that I'd show up for a blind date. I didn't expect a second date. I didn't even expect to have a good time.

"I'll tell her. I'm sure that'll make her feel better." Dad chuckled, and it was a good sound. "Talk to you later, sweetheart."

"Bye, Dad." I ended the call just in time. I blinked away my tears as Haley walked back into the room.

"Your ice cream concoction. I don't know how you eat

them together. That's kind of gross." Haley held out the bowl, her face scrunched up.

"Thanks. I need the sugar. I figure that after having a fireman see all the extra cookies and ice cream packed on my thighs, I don't have to worry about it anymore. Lightning doesn't strike twice."

"That doesn't sound so convincing coming from someone who had lightning strike their house and had a tree fall on them within a really short time frame."

"Those two things are completely different."

"You keep telling yourself that." Haley turned her phone to show me a picture. "Remember Zach Gallagher?"

"That's not Zach."

"Of course that's not Zach. That's his fiancée." Haley had been crushing on her brother's best friend since her sophomore year of high school. Maybe even before that, but we didn't know each other then.

"She's stunning. You're friends with Zach now? When did that happen?"

"I'm not friends with him. I'm friends with her. She's my new neighbor."

"Oh. Sorry."

"What's to be sorry about? I'm happy for him. I'd never go out with him. I mean, he treats me like I'm ten and still calls me *Carrot*. Besides, if I went out with Zach—not that he's remotely interested—my brother would never speak to me again." She attacked the last bit of ice cream in her bowl.

"Carrot?"

She pointed at her hair.

"Have you bumped into him?"

"Nah. And hopefully it stays that way." Haley dropped her spoon into the empty dish. "I know it's early, but I'm tired. Don't hate me for bailing on you."

"I'm fine. Go sleep." I pulled the blanket up without disturbing Pookie. "Goodnight."

She switched off the light and wandered down the hall.

In the dark, when I closed my eyes, the tree fell onto the tub over and over. Adam swooped in to rescue me every time, sometimes without a shirt on, which made no sense at all. In the wee hours of the morning, while Pookie tore through the apartment chasing phantoms, I inhaled the scent of my fireman and drifted off to sleep.

Tomorrow, I would put on a clean shirt.

CHAPTER 3

I opened my eyes when Haley nudged my hip. "What?"

"Here's coffee. You need to get up. It's almost noon. We have to go get your car, and you need to figure out what to wear tonight."

"And I need to buy a yellow rose." I sat up and sipped the coffee. "I'll see what I have to wear on the blind date. That was the last thing on my mind last night."

"Please don't wear that t-shirt. It's covered in dog hair." Haley shook her head. "Typical guy."

I picked short brown hairs and a few white hairs off the shirt. "Sorry. I hadn't noticed. And I wasn't planning to wear this." I set my suitcase on the coffee table and laid it open. "I'm not even sure what's clean and what needs to be washed."

"That's because you're a mess. I can't believe he picked up your stuff off the floor."

"Ugh. Don't remind me."

"You have quite a bit of lace in there. I wonder if he noticed that when he was stuffing clothes into the case."

"I also have the kind of undergarments you think no one will ever see. He probably noticed those. And it doesn't matter what he noticed because I'll probably never see him again."

"He was cute though." Haley sighed. "If you like the muscular, gorgeous type." Why had I let her anywhere near my house when the firemen were still there?

"Mind if I wash a load?" I didn't want to talk about the muscular and good-looking Adam Cardona.

"Be my guest."

"After that, we can go get my car. Then I'll run by my house and find a dress. Pants aren't going to feel good rubbing against my stitches."

Haley twisted her red curls into a knot and pinned them up with a clip. "I know you don't have high hopes for this date because—hello—your mom set you up, but isn't there a small part of you that hopes it works out?"

I pulled the dirty clothes out of my suitcase. "I haven't really thought about it. My life isn't bad. It's not like I *need* someone."

"You just *need* your mom to understand that."

"I'm not going to hold my breath." With an armload of clothes, I headed for the washer. "At least maybe tonight will help me forget about the horror of yesterday. It can serve as a diversion."

Haley grinned when I walked back into the living room. "Maybe you should take cookies to the fire station, as a—you know—thank-you-for-saving-me gesture."

"But that would make not seeing that fireman again more difficult. I'm aiming for *never*." I closed myself into the bathroom as much to get ready to go as to end the conversation.

Haley knocked.

"What?" I didn't open the door.

"You'll need this plastic wrap for your leg if you plan to take a shower. They said to keep the stitches dry."

"I'll shower when I get back."

∾

Clutching my single yellow rose, I sat on a bench near the door, bouncing my knee. Why was I nervous about a date I was sure wouldn't go well?

I'd insisted on being the one with the flower because if the guy wasn't interested in spending the evening with me, he could just keep walking. I half expected to sit here for a while then leave because my date never showed up.

Waiting, I ran my finger along the carvings in the wooden bench. While some could be attributed to ill-behaved children, others were clearly done by people older than five. What kind of people carved their names into benches?

At two minutes before six, a tall, lanky guy swooped into the room. He had a slight resemblance to Gumby, except he wasn't green. He smiled as if maybe he was about to walk over, but then he spotted someone already seated at a table and waved.

I went back to inspecting the carvings. Did Rob still love Angie? Why did Neil feel the need to let the world know he'd been here?

Right at six, a group of three guys walked in. If my date had brought friends along, I wasn't staying. Two of them had their ball caps on not completely backward. I didn't understand that. Were they trying to keep the sun off the space behind their ear?

Those guys weren't my type. And to prove it, they snickered when they spotted the rose. I might as well have been wearing a t-shirt that read *Laugh at me. I'm on a blind date*.

By three minutes past the hour, I thought about who had

walked in but didn't stop. It was looking more and more like I'd been stood up. But I promised myself I'd stay at the restaurant until ten minutes after six. At eleven minutes past the hour, I would assume I'd been stood up or ditched.

At seven minutes after, the door swung open and a bouquet of yellow roses blocked the face of whoever carried them. It seemed a tad coincidental. I was momentarily impressed. Then the flowers lowered.

Adam's gaze cut straight to my rose then snapped to my face. Eyebrows raised, he glanced down at his bouquet. Finally, after what felt like a year, he smiled.

Enduring a blind date with a guy who'd already seen me covered only in leaves was not on my bucket list. Forcing a smile, I stood—which was a feat all its own because my legs felt like they were made of jelly. Then I brushed past him and walked right out the door.

I could spend the evening digging up Thanksgiving recipes and watching videos about how to cook a turkey.

My mistake became obvious when I got to my car. My keys were in my purse, which was still sitting on the bench inside the restaurant. Dang, the man was distracting.

Hoping Adam had somehow disappeared into thin air, I turned . . . and bumped into him.

"Sorry I was late." He held the one thing keeping me from leaving. "You left your purse."

I snatched it out of his hand and grabbed my keys. "Thanks."

As I opened the car door, he touched my arm. "Just because I'm curious. Are you embarrassed or disappointed?"

How could the man think I was disappointed? I'd wager a guess that more than one girl had chased his firetruck down the street just to get a second look at him.

"Are you serious?" I slammed the door. "Twenty-four hours ago, I was in a *bathtub*."

"I remember. I was there too." Humor lit up those soft brown eyes.

My resolve to leave was slipping. "You moonlight as a comedian?"

"Nah. When I'm not saving people, I relax or go on blind dates." He held out the roses. "These are for you even if you decide to leave."

I did a quick count because I'm weird that way. "Eleven?"

"I thought it would be cute. The extra one is in my truck." He kicked at the ground. "It was nice meeting you, Eve."

"I'll stay." My tongue was a traitor. Salvaging control was only possible if I acted quickly. "But I have two rules: one—we don't talk about what happened, and two—your eyes stay up here." I circled my face with my finger because simply pointing didn't seem emphatic enough.

Immediately, he broke the second rule. Looking at my leg, he rubbed the back of his neck. "Did you get it looked at? Is it hurting?"

"Yes, I had it looked at, and yes, it hurts, and no, you can't see it." I adjusted my dress to be sure my wound was covered. "Now can we stick to the rules?"

A slow smile cut across his face, revealing dimples. "For the record, I prefer that my eyes stay in my face. If my eyes were on your face, I wouldn't be able to see you."

Despite my best efforts, I laughed. Hard. Picturing my face with two eyeballs glued to my cheek kicked off another minute of laughter. When I caught my breath, I smiled. "Sorry I walked out. I'm only here because my mom threatened to make me host holiday dinners. I was expecting some slightly awkward academic type. Not you."

"I have so many questions, but maybe we should get a table first." He held out his arm.

I looped my arm through his and nonchalantly assessed the size of his bicep. "Thanks for the roses."

"Thanks for staying. I figure this might be kinda fun because it won't be all weird. We've gotten that part out of the way." He held open the door.

"Are you forgetting the rules?"

"I meant in the parking lot." He lifted his eyebrows, humor etched on his face. "Just now."

The hostess seated us in a corner booth. And I acted like I didn't notice her checking out my date.

The tall backs on the wooden benches made it feel very private. I bet people had carved on these benches too.

He scanned the cowboy-themed décor. "I hope this place is okay."

"It's great. I love coming here." I tucked my feet close to my bench so I didn't accidentally bump him. It was way too soon for that.

He leaned back and crossed his arms, extending his legs all the way to my side. "You expected someone different?"

I may have intentionally bumped my foot against his just to gauge his reaction. "Very." I knew better than to ask the same question. I was almost thirty, still single, and had a cat. I was likely exactly who he expected to meet on a blind date.

Those dimples appeared again.

His gaze warmed me down to my toes, but it also made me self-conscious.

Why was I still holding the roses? "I think there are some basic questions we're supposed to cover." I nestled the bouquet next to me on the bench seat. "I'll start. Do you go on a lot of blind dates?"

"This is my second." He picked up his menu.

I always ordered the same thing at this restaurant, and I saw no point in changing my mind this time. I pushed the menu aside. "I'm guessing it didn't go amazingly since you are here."

"We went to a concert. She showed up drunk, started

hollering at the band, and was asked to leave the venue. So no, it didn't go well."

"That's horrible."

After an experience that bad, it was a little surprising he agreed to another blind date.

He closed his menu. "And because of that, I almost said no when my mom wanted to set me up again."

"Again? Wow. You're a brave guy." Telling that to a guy who ran into burning buildings was funny. So I laughed.

"And you're laughing at me." His smile betrayed the distressed tone.

"Oh no. I'm laughing at me, but I do that a lot. How does your mom know my mom?"

He shrugged. "Is hosting holiday dinner such a horrible thing?"

"If I have to cook for everyone, yes. And they stay for hours." I'd done it once right after I purchased the house and swore never to do it again. Even then, I didn't prepare all the food. Mom helped.

Adam chuckled. "You say that as if you've lived it before."

"I have. *Once*." Where was the waitress? I needed something to sip while chatting, something to hold onto.

Adam scanned the room. "If they ever let us order, I'll buy you dinner."

Just then a waitress hurried up. "So sorry. I didn't realize this table was part of my section. It's only my second day." She flipped open an ordering pad. "My name is Suzy. I'll be your server today."

He nodded toward me. "What would you like?"

I ordered, thinking that I'd very much like to go on a second date.

CHAPTER 4

Walking to my car, I ran through the possible ways the date could end. Conversation during dinner never dragged, and I'd managed to keep soda from coming out my nose when Adam made me laugh—and he'd done that a lot. He'd earned a check plus in the humor column.

But he wasn't without his quirks. When his plate arrived at the table, he moved the mashed potatoes—which he ordered without gravy—away from the steak and the green beans away from the mashed potatoes. If keeping food separate was his biggest flaw, I could live with that.

Would he ask me out again? I wanted him to.

Would he kiss me?

Did I want him to? *Yes, please*.

When we arrived at my car, he handed over the roses. "This has been fun."

"I agree." I tucked the roses into the backseat so that my hands were empty. Would he correctly interpret my strategy?

Once I closed the door, he leaned against my car. And he

was one of those men that had mastered that move. With his arms crossed, muscles stretched the sleeves of his shirt.

I forced myself not to inch closer. "I'm glad you stopped me."

"I'm glad you changed your mind about leaving." He moved closer. "Any chance you'd want to have dinner with me again?"

"I could be talked into that." I crossed my arms, unsure what to do with my empty hands, but then thought better of it. I didn't want to send signals that I was putting up a wall.

"I'll pick you up, which would save you money on gas. Dinner will be on me, which saves you money. You have to eat, right? And I'll let you choose the place." He lifted one eyebrow.

"Is that you talking me into it?"

"Is it working?"

I nodded then shook my head. "But I don't want to choose."

"If I must, I will force my choice upon you." He slipped his phone out of his pocket. "If I'm going to pick you up and arrange for dinner, I'll need your number."

Making sure my fingers brushed his, I took his phone and added my info. "I'll let you name the contact."

"See, that's where a really good joke could get me in all kinds of trouble. There are rules." He grabbed his phone and my hand with it. "Are there any rules against a goodnight kiss?"

"No." I didn't want him to think I was saying no to the kiss, so I quickly added, "There are no rules against that."

He tugged me closer. "I'm happy to hear that."

When he bent forward, my eyes slipped closed as I anticipated the feel of his lips on mine. And he did not disappoint. His lips moved against mine, and his very muscular arm circled my waist.

He didn't linger long enough to make people stare, but it was long enough to send my heartrate skyrocketing.

To think I'd almost left.

When he broke away, he stayed close, his mouth hovering inches from mine. "I should probably say goodnight, but I don't want to."

I tried to tame my smile so I didn't resemble the Cheshire cat. And it was definitely not the right time to toy with the buttons on his shirt. Not that I wanted him to take it off or anything, but I liked being close to him. And nervous energy made the urge to fidget almost uncontrollable. "I completely understand."

Just as he closed the distance and touched his lips to mine once again, my phone buzzed in my pocket. I ignored it.

When his phone started buzzing, we both laughed.

"What would you wager that my mother is calling to ask about my date?" With his arm still around me, he turned the phone so that I could see that his guess was correct.

"I'm guessing my mom just called me for the same reason. And for the record, I'm not telling her about this last part."

Adam winked. "Good to know." He opened my car door. "Be careful driving home."

Since he wasn't on duty, ready to come to my rescue, I'd be doubly careful. But out loud, I only said a portion of that. "I will." Letting my hand slip out of his, I climbed into the car. "'Night."

He closed the door and did that double tap thing. He definitely had the guy things down: the lean, the double tap, the kiss. The other guys I'd dated had missed those training days apparently.

As soon as I shifted into reverse, my phone rang again. Mom would continue to call until I answered, so I put the car back in park and answered, faking my best sleepy voice. "Hello."

"Did I wake you? You're in bed already? Was the date that bad? Mrs. Cardona said her son was good looking. She thought you two would get along."

I giggled, letting Mom in on my joke.

"Ay! Why do you tease your mother? I only do this because I care about you."

"I know, Mom." I scanned the lot and stifled a laugh when I spotted Adam sitting in his truck and talking on the phone. "We just left the restaurant. I was just about to drive back to Haley's."

"This hotel suite has two bedrooms. You can stay here with us."

"I'm fine at Haley's. Thanks though." I shifted the phone to my other ear so I could spy on Adam while I talked. "He was very nice. A complete gentleman."

Besides being good looking, those were the things that mattered to my mother. Haley would hear about his other qualities.

"Did he pay for dinner?"

"He did."

"Are you going to go out with him again?" Mom had all the hope of a kid whispering their wish to Santa.

"If he calls me, yes." Carefully worded, my answer wasn't untrue.

A gleeful giggle sounded from the other end of the line. "I'll call you back later."

"Please tell me you aren't going to call Mrs. Cardona."

"Bye, Eve. Be careful driving." Mom ended the call.

And if I had any doubt about what she was doing, that was erased when Adam hung up a minute later. He waved before backing out.

So far, I liked Adam, but being set up by our mothers could prove to be a problem.

When I got back to the apartment, Haley met me at the door. "Your mom has called twice."

"Why did she call you? And when?"

"I assume because you didn't answer. About twenty minutes ago."

I dropped my purse and dug through my suitcase. I'd washed his t-shirt, but maybe there would be a hint of him still caught in the threads. "Let me change really quick, then I'll tell you all about it."

"Popcorn or ice cream? And both is not an acceptable answer."

"Popcorn."

"Is that because you're feeling salty or because you've overdosed on sweet?"

"You'll have to wait until after I change clothes to find out the answer." I tossed the t-shirt over my shoulder and headed for the bathroom.

"Since you're putting that fireman's shirt on, I'm guessing your date bombed."

"You know what assuming does." I'd have fun telling her about my date.

The scent of butter filled the apartment, and I snuggled into my favorite spot at the end of the sofa. "You want the short version or the long version?"

"The long version, of course. Here." Haley handed over a bowl and plopped onto the other end of the sofa. "Spill it."

"The long version has parts I'm not ready to tell my mom."

Haley dragged a finger along her lips. "She won't hear it from me."

"At six, he hadn't shown up, and I was ready to bolt. A few minutes after, Adam walked in—"

"No! What did his date look like?"

"He didn't have a date, but he was carrying eleven yellow roses."

Her jaw fell open. Then she squealed. "It went well. That's why you are wearing his shirt."

"You're interrupting my story."

"Sorry. Keep talking."

I popped a couple of pieces of popcorn in my mouth, making her wait. "When he walked in, I walked out. After the way he saw me in the tub, I wasn't about to stay."

"Then what have you been doing for these last four hours?"

"This is taking much longer than it needs to." I licked butter off my fingers. The movie theater kind of popcorn was my favorite.

Haley shook her head. "You're maddening."

"Anyway, I walked out without my purse. He brought it to me. And he asked if I was embarrassed or disappointed."

"The way he looks, no way. Unless he's a snot in person."

"He's not. He's charming and funny. And a great kisser."

Haley jumped up and did a little dance. "I'm so happy for you. This is awesome, and I won't tell your mom about the kiss."

"Thank you. Our second kiss was interrupted by our moms."

"That'll make dating complicated. I am a bit surprised though."

"Surprised? Why?"

"You can't stand dogs. I thought you swore that you'd *never* date a guy with a dog."

"He didn't say anything about a dog."

Haley snapped her fingers in front of my face. "Hello! Dog hair on the shirt. That seems like a big clue."

"Maybe one of the other guys in the crew has a dog. That would explain it."

"I'll bet you one week of dish duty that he has at least one dog."

I knew better than to take that bet, but again my body betrayed me. My hand flew out to shake on the deal, and my tongue agreed. "It's a bet."

CHAPTER 5

While staying at Haley's was minimally better than staying at my parents', the fact that Haley woke up bright-eyed and bubbly made life rough. I liked to slowly come to terms with the loss of night then sip coffee in silence until I was ready to start the day.

And the two of us sharing one bathroom wasn't working out so well. I pulled my hair into a ponytail. Hopefully no one at work would notice that it hadn't been washed that morning.

"See you tonight, Haley."

"Want me to pick up dinner?"

"I'll make something. Text me when you decide what sounds good." I cuddled Pookie before walking out the door then brushed cat fur off my blouse.

Surely a little bit of dog hair didn't mean Adam had a mangy beast. It wasn't that I hated dogs. I didn't. I just . . . Who wanted to be toppled by a beast or have one sit on their head? Not me. Something I didn't admit to anyone was that deep inside, I was afraid of them. Little dogs always seemed high strung and out of sorts. Big dogs—well, they were the topple and sit-on-your-head types. And the licking. I couldn't handle the licking.

But dwelling on what furry friends Adam had wasn't time well spent.

My mom's perfect sense of timing made me wonder if she'd planted a mini camera in my purse. I'd just climbed into the car when she called.

"Hey, Mom."

"Eve, hi. I was hoping to catch you before you got into the office."

"I was just about to leave."

"Oh, good. Put the speaker on. You can't hold the phone while you drive. You'll get a ticket."

"Yes, Mom." I'd fought the urge to call her all day Sunday because I didn't want to seem desperate for information. But truly, I was almost to that point. What had Mrs. Cardona told Mom that had gotten passed from Adam? "What's up?" My ability to sound casual impressed even me.

"Do you want to know what Mrs. Cardona said?" Was Mom seriously making me admit I wanted to know. Of course she was.

"Sure."

"I'm surprised you didn't call me yesterday. I told you I was going to call her."

"I still can't believe you called her so late on Saturday. And I figured if there was anything I needed to know, you'd call me."

"Are you paying attention to the road? I don't want to distract you."

"I'm watching the road."

"All right. So, I called Mrs. Cardona after I talked to you on Saturday." Mom often introduced her stories with facts I already knew. "Mandy is such a nice lady. She's in my book club. Have I mentioned her before?" Chasing tangents was another common element of Mom's stories.

"I don't remember that name."

"I love when she suggests a book. I haven't disliked a single one. But when Lulu Meyers gives a suggestion, I'm almost guaranteed not to like it. Anyway, back to what Mandy said."

Traffic inched along, and I held my breath, hoping Mom would spill what she knew without me having to ask again.

"Adam didn't say much to her. He said you were nice." She sighed as if the news was disappointing. "I told her that he paid for dinner and that he was a gentleman. She was happy to hear that. I don't know anything else about what Adam thought of the date. She did say he hadn't dated in a while. So maybe he isn't as great as his mother thinks he is."

I turned into the lot and found a place to park. Telling my mom that he was a great kisser would guarantee that his mom heard that tidbit. Whether or not she'd pass that on to Adam was questionable. Shocking Mom wasn't worth the risk of fallout from saying that. "Well, I thought he was nice."

Nice was one of those words that could be used as a compliment or a slap-down. It gave my mother only a little drop of info, and when it filtered to Adam, hopefully he'd interpret the word correctly.

"Good. Well, I hope you aren't too disappointed if he doesn't call you." Mom's vote of confidence was heartwarming.

"I'm fine either way." That wasn't exactly true. I'd be a little bummed if he never called, but I wasn't about to let that slip to Mom. "I just got to work, so I need to run."

"Okay, dear. Have a good day. Oh! When will your house be finished?"

"Hopefully at the end of the week. But I'm not holding my breath." Because we were dangerously close to a question I didn't want her to ask, I wrapped up the call. "I'll talk to you later. Bye."

For now, I'd dodged the question. But I knew how it felt to be displaced. Mom and Dad would be out of their house for weeks, maybe months. I had two extra bedrooms at my house. Thinking about that now would only make Monday more difficult, so the whole housing status got pushed back to tomorrow's worry list.

~

THAT AFTERNOON, I TRUDGED BACK OUT TO MY CAR. WHY HAD I volunteered to make dinner? I just wanted to pick up food from a drive-thru, get into pajama pants and a t-shirt—probably something other than Adam's shirt—and mindlessly watch television.

But I wanted to be a good houseguest and a good friend. I climbed into the car and pulled out my phone. Haley hadn't texted all day. Maybe sharing the apartment was too much for her. As I was tapping out a message to her, another popped up. I didn't even finish typing.

Adam had texted: *Nice, huh? Maybe I'll shoot for really nice on our next date.*

Really nice isn't an easy achievement. I hoped none of my coworkers walked by and saw me grinning at my phone.

Could I buy you dessert and coffee tonight and maybe get the scoop on what I'd need to do to unlock that achievement?

Waiting a second or two was probably the coy way to handle the question. I typed so fast my fingers got tangled. *Yes. Absolutely.*

What if I pick you up at eight?

Perfect. I'm staying with my friend. I'll send over the address. See you later.

I'm looking forward to it. And I was. Immensely.

I sent over the address then texted Haley. *Leaving work now. Will start dinner as soon as I get home.*

Don't bother. New client. I'm working late. Sorry. She loved her job, but it could take over her life sometimes.

No worries. Talk to you later.

Having a few hours to myself before dessert wasn't a bad thing at all.

I drove home and picked up tacos on the way. But I was mostly on autopilot because I was trying to figure out what to wear. If I was too dressed up, I'd look like I was trying too hard, but too casual would signal that I didn't care all that much. Why did I make things so complicated?

After eating and getting ready, my few hours felt like minutes. It was nearly eight, but Haley hadn't made it home. I scribbled out a note letting her know I'd gone out for coffee and dessert. I laid Adam's t-shirt on the table and set the note on top.

A minute later, someone knocked.

A deep breath calmed my nerves, and I opened the door. "Hi."

"Hey. You look nice." His gaze dropped to Pookie who was batting at my shoes. "Hey there, Pookie. You staying out of trees?" Adam rubbed the back of his neck.

He didn't pet my cat. Normally his kitten avoidance would be a red flag, but Pookie had scratched him, so I forgave him for not petting my kitty. This time. "Scratches still hurt?"

"Only a little. But we aren't going to talk about any of that."

If he kept up this level of charm, I'd have to create yet another tier.

"Right. But I am sorry she hurt you." I locked the apartment door.

"Seeing you again is easing the pain." Grinning, Adam let

his fingers brush against mine as we walked out to the truck. "I had dinner plans with my family tonight, or I would've suggested dinner."

"I never turn down dessert."

Great. Now he probably thought I was a pig who stuffed my face with multiple helpings of dessert every night.

"And I would have invited you to dinner, but I'm not quite ready to have our moms in the middle of things any more than they already are."

"I agree."

After helping me into the truck, he started the engine. "Cheesecake or pie?"

"That's a hard question. With pie, there are so many options. And I love a warm slice of apple or a chilled slice of lemon meringue. But cheesecake has a certain satisfying creaminess."

"Cheesecake it is then." He winked.

When we stopped outside the restaurant, I grabbed his hand getting out of the truck and saw no reason to let go even after he closed the door.

Things were definitely moving in the right direction.

The waitress sat us at a table for two. I ordered a decadent slice that I knew would come drenched in chocolate, caramel, and other goodness. Adam ordered plain cheesecake. He didn't even want any strawberry topping.

Maybe this relationship didn't have a future.

CHAPTER 6

Thursday evening, I flopped on the sofa, and Pookie jumped into my lap. "Where did you order from? This pizza is really good."

Haley dropped into the overstuffed chair. "It's good because I didn't have them put weird stuff on it. Who wants bell pepper touching their sausage or black olives crowding out the pepperoni?"

"Not you apparently. But I like this meat extravaganza. It's tasty." I finished off my slice, keeping it out of Pookie's reach because she wasn't great at staying away from food that drifted too close to her face. "Derek called today. I'm doing a final walkthrough tomorrow. He said everything at the house should be done by five."

"Awesome. Don't get me wrong. I like having you around, but the bathroom is getting smaller by the day."

"I agree. And I'm ready to be back in my own place." I popped the last bite of crust in my mouth. "Do you think I should invite my parents to stay at my house until their place is repaired?"

Bits of pepperoni and cheese flew out of Haley's mouth as she laughed. "That's funny."

"I wasn't trying to be funny. I feel a bit guilty because now I have a house and they don't. They offered me a place to live when my house was damaged."

She picked up another slice. "Think about it before you ask. It would be nice, and I'm sure they would accept, after making you offer two or three times. But, honestly, would you be okay with that?"

I really wanted to go home to my own space and settle back into life as it was before the lightning strike. But guilt. "I think the guilt of not offering would eat me alive."

"Don't say I didn't warn you."

"I know. I know."

Pookie seemed to know I needed soothing and climbed up onto my shoulder. Either that or she knew I was about to grab another slice of pizza.

Haley sighed. That was her typical way of getting my attention before fussing at me.

"What?" Eyebrows raised, I gave her my questioning look with a bit of added drama.

She set her pizza down. "Are you ever going to tell me how your second date went?"

"Oh. I wasn't trying to keep things from you. You were asleep when I got home, and you've worked late every night this week."

"All right already. Just tell me."

I finished my slice, driving my best friend mad with impatience. "We had a nice time. I didn't mention anything about moving back home. I mean, I only have my suitcase and the cat, but I was not about to talk about moving to a guy with a truck. We are definitely not at that point in the relationship."

"Relationship? That sounds serious."

"Did you just hear me? I didn't even tell him about moving. We've only gone out twice."

"He didn't wait very long to call again. I think that means something."

"It probably means his mom was bugging him about me." I said that, but I didn't really believe it because my mom hadn't called. My guess was that he hadn't mentioned the date to his mom.

While we finished off the pizza, I gave Haley all the details about the date.

"Ignoring the fact that he ordered plain cheesecake, would you go out with him again?"

"Yes."

"Have you heard from him since dessert?"

"I have. It seems we've moved to the phase of exchanging texts for no reason."

"Oooh, so quickly. You haven't even known him a week. Well, I guess tomorrow will be a week."

"We don't count tomorrow." I hadn't filled Haley in on the rules.

"You may not count it, but I assure you, he hasn't forgotten. So now for the big question. You'll date this guy even though he has a dog?" Haley grabbed a few kitty treats and dropped them one at a time when Pookie sat up to beg. "Isn't this cute?"

The little cat caught each treat between her paws.

"When did you teach her to do that? That's awesome."

"Don't ignore my question." Haley signed 'all done,' and Pookie scurried back toward me. "As long as I've known you, you swore you wouldn't date a guy with a dog."

"You taught my cat sign language?"

Haley shrugged. "You think his dog is that smart?"

"He hasn't said anything about a dog."

She shook her head. "You are playing in dangerous territory. What if you fall head over heels and then meet his mangy dog? What then?"

"I think he would have mentioned if he had a dog." I hadn't asked about his dog because I didn't want to hear the answer.

Haley's question was a bit unsettling.

"And I'm far from falling in love."

She yawned and picked up the pizza box. "You say that now."

"Don't worry. If everything falls apart because of a dog, I'll remember that you told me so."

"Good." She waved as she walked down the hall. "'Night."

CHAPTER 7

Maybe I was a bit superstitious, but I didn't take the afternoon off. The last time I'd done that to check on repairs my day hadn't ended well. Not that meeting Adam was a bad thing. I just wished I'd been wearing more—shoot, anything—when we met for the first time.

I planned my day so that I could leave the office a little bit early, but by mid-morning I was almost too distracted to think. A text from Adam only compounded that.

Happy Friday. Big plans for the weekend?

Moving back into my house! Thankfully, it doesn't involve a moving truck. I only have to drag furniture out of the guest rooms back into the master suite.

Need a strong guy to help?

Sure. Know any? I made sure to follow my text with a laughing emoji. *I'd love your help.*

Love was probably too strong a word, but not having to drag my king-size mattresses across the house alone was worth the overstep. My twenty-year-old self would never have joked like that or used that word one week into a relationship. But my almost-thirty-year-old self had a better appreciation for humor—even if I was the only one who thought it was funny—and I wasn't afraid to speak my mind. I still had a filter, so not everything spewed out of my mouth thankfully.

I'm free tonight and tomorrow. Then I'm back on duty.

I'll text you as soon as I know the house is ready.

Great. I'll bring dinner. He was really scoring points.

You're the best.

He replied as I was about to put down my phone. *Wow! You skipped over really nice.*

I sent a wink as a reply then tried to get some work done. But since my brain only wanted to think about a certain fireman, productivity was a lost cause.

∽

RACING OUT OF THE OFFICE A HALF HOUR EARLY, I PRAYED traffic wouldn't be horrible.

Pulling into my own driveway was a treat. The work trucks were gone, so either the guys were finished or they'd left early to start the weekend. I truly hoped it wasn't the latter.

Derek's truck rumbled up to the curb right on time, and excitement bubbled in my chest. Almost two months out of my house felt like forever.

The keys dangling off his belt loop jingled as he walked to the door. "I can't wait for you to see it. Everything turned out great."

"No more pink bathroom?"

"No more pink." He followed me into the master suite. "What do you think?"

Last time I'd been here, the floors were bare concrete and

the bedroom hadn't been painted. Now, the room looked like a page out of a magazine.

"This is amazing. I love it." I hurried into the bathroom, which now had the correct color on the walls. "This all turned out so wonderful. You did a great job."

"Thank you." He checked his phone. Derek did that a lot.

"So this is it? I can move back in?"

"Anytime you want. We're finished." He handed me the bill.

I paid the man, knowing how I'd be spending my evening. I couldn't wait to move back in.

Once Derek left, I called Haley. "It's done! The floors are in. The roof is fixed. The walls are painted. It's all mine."

"Until your parents move in."

"You couldn't even let me have my moment?"

Haley laughed. "Sorry."

"You don't sound the least bit sorry. I'm headed to the apartment to grab my stuff and Pookie. Then Adam is meeting me at the house."

"Is he bringing his dog?" Laughing, Haley ended the call.

If Adam did own a dog, I was never going to hear the end of it.

I texted Adam before leaving for the apartment: *It's finished. I'm running to the apartment to get Pookie and my suitcase, but I'll be back here soon.*

Where is here? 6:30 okay?

I sent off my address. *6:30 is great.*

If I was going to do what I needed to do and be back in time to meet Adam, I needed to hurry. I stopped at the store and bought flowers and chocolates as a thank you for Haley.

Pookie greeted me at the door when I made it to the apartment.

"Are you ready to go home, fuzzy? You get to see Adam again tonight. Please be nice."

She meowed, which hopefully meant she was assuring me of good behavior.

After getting everything packed and loaded, I made it back to the house with fifteen minutes to spare. So when Adam arrived right on time, I appeared calm and collected.

He held up the bag with the logo from a local barbeque joint emblazoned on the side. "Where should I put this?"

"Kitchen is this way. Thanks for bringing food."

"My pleasure." He set the bag on the counter. "Your house is nice."

"Thanks. I really appreciate your help." As I put food on plates, I nodded toward the fridge. "I picked up Cokes. Want one?"

"Sounds great." He moved the plates to the table. "You said lightning hit the house, right?" He waited until I sat down before taking his seat.

His manners almost made me want to curtsey.

"Yes. It hit the garage which is next to my bedroom. Copper pipe in the foundation burst. It put a hole in the roof and in the front of the house. I was out of the house for almost two months while that was all fixed. But thankfully, the place didn't catch fire."

"It's a good thing because a different station responds to calls for this neighborhood. I wouldn't have been here to save you like I was a week ago." He winked.

"Are you forgetting the rules?"

"I thought women liked it when men remembered anniversaries and special days."

"We do." I reached out and grabbed his hand. "It makes us feel special. Unless that special day was the worst one of our life."

"But I saved you."

His flagrant disregard for rule one earned him a kiss, and I temporarily forgot about the food.

Adam brushed a thumb along my cheek. "I'm glad we met on that blind date."

"Me too. And I'm glad I didn't leave." I turned back to the table just in time to see Pookie drag the meat off Adam's plate. "Kitty, you were supposed to behave."

My cat was out to ruin my evening.

"If she eats all that, it'll make her sick." I didn't even want to think about cleaning up after her.

Adam reached down to take the stolen food away and was rewarded with razor-sharp claws. He yanked his hand back, but not before Pookie sliced open his finger. His jaw clenched. "I'll just let you handle it."

I scooped up Pookie and tossed her in the guest room. "How could you?"

She flicked her tail and climbed up onto the bed. Closing her into the room wasn't much of a punishment. I hurried back to the kitchen. "Oh, Adam, I'm so sorry. Let me get something to put on that."

While he assured me it wasn't a big deal, I grabbed bandages and antibiotic cream. "Here, let me see that."

Rough and calloused, his hand was much bigger than mine. And it was warm. Not he-has-a-fever warm but the I-bet-they'd-feel-good-against-my-skin kind of warm. I hadn't invested so much thought on his hands since one was brushing against my thigh a week ago. If I let my thoughts wander there, my whole body would flush pink.

After smoothing the bandage so that the edges stayed down, I dropped a quick kiss on his finger. "I can probably find someone else to help me move if that hurts."

"Do you always buy Band-Aids with cats on them?"

"They're cute, aren't they?"

"Just what I've always wanted: a cute Band-Aid." He wasn't laughing, so hopefully he didn't mind too much. "Don't call anyone else. I'll live, but only if I eat."

I served him more food on a clean plate. "I am sorry about that. She usually doesn't do that."

"Lucky me."

Forty-five minutes later, I tossed dishes in the sink and set the leftover food in the fridge. "There isn't a whole lot. Mainly, a bed and a dresser. And a bookshelf."

His eyebrow arched. "And?"

I really wanted to be able to say that was it, but I remembered my hope chest. There was no way I was calling it that in front of him because I didn't want to sound desperate. "My cedar chest, but that's on wheels so I can move that whenever."

"I've always wondered what women keep in those. My mom has one, but she always calls it her hope chest."

"We keep our hopes in them. Duh."

"Of course." He chuckled then stepped closer and brushed a finger along my hand. "Now I really want a peek inside."

I really liked this guy, and if I could get my cat to stop drawing blood, the relationship had a real chance of blossoming into more. "We'll see." I hoped my answer sounded coy and not dismissive.

But if he expected anything salacious to be hiding in that chest, he'd be disappointed. In my chest were blankets and a quilt my grandmother had passed down to me.

He clapped his hands once as if he was kicking off a game. "Show me what to move."

I led him down the hall to the guest room. When I pushed the door open, Pookie dashed out, probably feeling victorious about her escape. "She hates being trapped." I pointed at the furniture shoved against the wall. "The stuff on this side goes into the master bedroom. Which is . . ." I walked to the opposite end of the house. "In here."

"This looks great."

"Oh! There's a rug in the garage. I need to put that out

first." I kept talking as I walked. "I should've been more together before calling you. I apologize for being scattered."

He caught my hand. "Don't apologize."

How was this guy still single? Was the visible layer of charming and nice covering something else entirely? If so, he had me fooled. All those thoughts sent my brain on a tangent. "How old are you?"

Grinning, his eyes narrowed. "I'll act like that question didn't come out of nowhere. I'm thirty-one."

"Okay. And I'll try to stop apologizing, but it's habit." I lived with the belief that I was somehow letting down the world one little bit at a time.

He pushed open the garage door. "Did you tell your mom I was coming over?"

"No. But it'll come up, I'm sure." I shifted out of the way as Adam dragged the rug into the bedroom.

"Why are you so sure of that? I haven't said anything to my mom either. Last she knew, I thought you were nice."

Moving the rug into place, I laughed. "Because when they come over to see this place, they'll ask why I didn't call them to help put the furniture back. And I will ignore the question, but Mom won't give up asking about it until I tell her the truth. That's why."

"That makes perfect sense. I can see why our moms get along." He disappeared down the hall and came back carrying the bed frame. "Any other random questions you want to ask me?"

With an invitation like that, I wasn't about to stand there quietly. "Have you ever been married?"

"Nope." He lay down on the floor and bolted pieces together. "Let me grab the headboard."

I followed him down the hall. "Serious girlfriends?"

"I guess that depends on your definition of serious."

"Were you ever engaged?"

"Came close once, but she broke it off before I asked. Thankfully, she broke it off before I bought a ring."

"What happened?"

"She wasn't crazy about my work schedule." He attached the headboard to the frame. "What about you?"

"I don't mind your work schedule. I mean, you're a firefighter. It's part of the fireman package."

He stepped toward me, and teasingly, I backed up until I was against the wall. His grin widened and he stepped closer.

"Fireman package?"

I could feel my cheeks on fire. "I just meant fireman package as in they go together. It's not like I—that's all I meant." Flustered, I was sure my face was flaming red.

Then he leaned in closer, and the tease in his tone was evident. "Makes perfect sense. I'm glad you don't mind my schedule, but I was asking if *you* had ever been engaged or married."

I inched closer. "I've never been married or engaged. I once dated a guy for six months. We had dinner with my parents one night—you know, so he could meet them. Mom asked if he wanted kids, and I never heard from the guy again."

"Ugh. Guys like that give the rest of us a bad name."

In a quick move, I stepped around him. "I called him a few of those bad names. I admit it."

Adam picked up one end of the box spring. I picked up the other, and together we maneuvered it down into the bedroom.

I wasn't done with asking random questions. "Do you hate Pookie?"

"I think maybe she hates me." He moved the mattress into place. "But no, I don't hate your adorably small, fuzzy, black kitten."

"Good." I did my best to hold up the end of the mattress as we moved it down the hall.

With his help, everything was moved in no time flat. Or maybe the conversation made time go faster.

"Have you always wanted to be a fireman?"

"Not always. When I was really little, I wanted to be Batman. I thought he was cooler than Superman or any of the others. Then when I was a bit older, I wanted to be a cowboy."

It took all my willpower not to ascertain how he filled out his Wranglers. But the fact that I knew he was wearing Wranglers meant I'd already glanced at his denim. "Why'd you give up on that plan? You have the boots and the truck."

"Considering I'd never been on a horse, I opted for something different."

"So you became a fireman."

"Right."

"Which is almost like Batman, but with less black."

His smile widened. "If that's you calling me a superhero, thanks."

"It was." Careful not to hit my toes, I lifted one end of the dresser. "Any siblings?"

"Two. They're both married, which makes me Mom's project."

"Anything else I should know about you before . . ." Why did I say before? There was no way to finish that sentence that wouldn't end in embarrassment.

His lips curled into a smile. "Before what?"

Maybe I could salvage the situation. "Before I roll my cedar chest down the hall."

"Do I get to look inside?"

Shaking my head, I stayed a few paces ahead of him. "Not tonight."

"To me that sounds like an invitation to come back again." He lifted his eyebrows.

"It is." My toe connected with the end of the dresser. "Yowch."

"You okay?"

"It was an extra toe. I'll be okay."

He helped me get everything into place. "What else can I do?"

"You've been a huge help. I'll take care of the rest. Have time for a cup of coffee?"

"I sure do." He stood extra close as I added water to the coffee pot. "You asked about other things you should know."

An icy chill scratched at my scalp and skittered down my arms. Rather than opening my mouth, I nodded.

"There is one thing." His drawn-out introduction was making my bones hurt.

"What? Just tell me already." My outburst surprised me. I sounded more like Haley.

He laughed. "I was hoping if I built it up enough the actual thing wouldn't seem like a big deal. Are you free tomorrow?"

"That one-hundred percent depends on what it is you need to say."

"I was hoping we could go to a park. I'd bring my dogs along, and we could walk the trails."

"Dogs plural, as in more than one?"

"Two. Butch and Sundance. I didn't mention them before because from our conversation on the day we never bring up, I got the strong impression you weren't a dog person."

Disappointment and fear rattled around inside me. If he'd mentioned dogs on our first date, would I have left? Again. That didn't much matter. Now, I was in the spot Haley warned me about. Maybe I wasn't exactly head over heels, but I was leaning that direction.

Feeling guilty that I couldn't just smile and act like the dogs were no big deal, I fought irritation that he hadn't told me before I'd become so charmed.

Ignoring the fact that I'd been quiet way too long, I met his gaze as I poured him a cup of steaming liquid. I rummaged through the jumble of words in my head, trying to choose the right ones to say.

He took a sip out of his mug and laughed.

"What's so funny?" I needed to get over myself, but his laughter didn't help. And I really didn't want to listen to Haley going on and on about being right.

He set his mug on the counter. "I'm laughing because there is no coffee in the coffee. You only ran water through the pot. And I probably should have mentioned my dogs sooner, but I was hoping that you'd like me enough that you'd give my dogs a chance."

"Are you always so . . . so honest?"

"Are we talking about when I didn't tell you or now?" He shoved a hand in his pocket.

Part of me wanted to be mad, but the other half of me wanted to kiss him. Staring at him, I tried to decide which urge to follow.

He ran his fingers through his hair. "I should probably go."

"But we haven't had coffee." I trailed a finger down his arm. "And, yes, I'm free tomorrow."

His eyes lit up, and that amazing smile cut across his face. "I'm really happy to hear that."

CHAPTER 8

The next day, as Adam's truck pulled into the lot, I sucked in a deep breath. "He's here."

Haley laughed. "When are you coming over to do my dishes?"

"Let them pile up for a week, then I'll come do them all at once."

When I ended the call, Haley was still laughing.

I climbed out of my car, not at all ready to meet his dogs. How had it come to this? Then Adam jumped out of the truck and smiled. I quickly remembered the reason. It wasn't just that he was good looking. He was, but there was also something magnetic about him.

"Hey there. I'm happy you showed up." He opened the back door and let the dogs jump down.

When he'd mentioned what breed of dogs they were, I'd researched. After searching and looking at pictures, I knew what kind of dogs they were. Big. That's what they were. And big dogs were the kind I disliked most.

As he attached the leash to the Husky, the other one—a Weimaraner, Adam had called it—bolted toward me, and in a split second, that dog had his paws on my shoulders and was licking my face.

Squeezing my mouth and eyes closed, I froze. Asking for help required opening my mouth, and I had no desire to get to know his dog that well.

"Whoa! Butch, get down. Stop kissing her. Down!" Adam grabbed the dog's collar. "I'm sorry. Are you okay?"

I wasn't going to be a wimp. "Yeah. I'm fine."

He pointed at the dogs, and they both sat obediently. "I'll have to make sure he knows that I'm the only one that gets to do that."

"It's a good thing you're so charming." I yanked the scrunchie off my wrist and pulled my hair into a ponytail.

He attached a leash to the kissing culprit. "This is Butch. And that's Sundance."

At the mention of their names, both dogs looked at Adam expectantly.

"They look eager to go." I smiled at them but kept my distance.

"Always." He held out his hand. "You ready?"

"Don't you need both hands for the leashes?" I reluctantly stepped close enough to grab his hand.

He clicked his tongue, and the dogs headed down the trail. "Despite Butch's earlier display, they're good dogs. I can hold both leashes in one hand."

"How long have you had these guys? Where did you get them?"

"I've had them two years. I got them both the same day from a local shelter." He gave my hand a quick squeeze. "I really am sorry."

"I don't hate dogs. I just don't like to be licked." This probably wasn't the best time to drop that tidbit.

"Fabulous." Concern echoed in his sarcasm.

"I guess that makes us even. Actually, you are still up one or two. My cat scratched you twice *and* stole your food."

"Such a sweet little creature."

"If you are willing to keep coming around and risk starvation and pain, I can deal with being licked."

"And you can tell him to stop. He does listen."

"Unlike Pookie."

"I wasn't going to bring that up." Adam chuckled. "Sleep well last night? I bet it was nice to be back in your own house again."

"Blissful, and I made sure to enjoy it because it isn't going to last. I'm going to invite my parents to stay while their house gets repaired. And that kind of affects you because . . ." I shrugged. "Do I really need to explain why?"

"Nope. Unless you start sneaking out of your own house and not telling your parents where you're headed, everyone will know when we see each other. I need to remember to never let my mom set me up again."

"I swore I'd never let my mom set me up. But after she begged me, I finally gave in." So far, I didn't regret it.

"And?"

"And I'm curious if you plan to go on another blind date anytime soon."

His brown eyes twinkled. "Not as long as you keep saying yes to going out with me."

"Gosh, if we stop dating, it might throw book club into chaos." I was quite sure both moms would blame me.

"We don't want to be responsible for that." He lurched forward as Sundance decided squirrels shouldn't be allowed on the trails. "Let it alone, boy. Don't tug my arm off."

"Who keeps them when you're working?"

"My housemate. Javi works from home, so these guys get plenty of attention." Adam stopped and faced me. "He's out of town visiting his girlfriend and won't be back until tomorrow. Would you maybe want to come over after this?"

We were up to seeing each other four times in one week. Five if you counted the rescue. Slowing down was probably wise. But my mouth had other ideas. "Sure. I can pick up lunch on the way." Caution, meet wind.

We turned around and headed back toward the parking lot.

Footsteps and jingling collars were the only sound for a little while. Adam still had his hand wrapped around mine, and I was glad I'd scratched one more never off my list.

"Penny for your thoughts."

"Not a chance." I grinned. "When are we going to go on a date that our mothers know about?"

"That makes us sound like teenagers who are sneaking around."

"I didn't sneak around when I was a teen. I was a model child."

"What happened?" That teasing grin creased his cheeks. "I'm on duty Friday and Saturday. We can do Thursday night or Sunday night, whichever works better for you."

"Thursday, with maybe an option for Sunday too. Is that asking too much?"

He stopped and snaked his arm around my waist. "Not in the least."

I tilted my head back, and as he leaned closer, my eyes slipped closed. His lips danced against mine, and dog fur brushed the back of my legs.

Laughing, he broke the kiss. "Looks like we're stuck like this."

His dogs had circled us, wrapping us in the leashes.

"What a shame." I grabbed his shirt as the dogs shifted and I tipped backward.

"I'll save you." Adam winked and smiled down at me. "Again."

∼

AFTER KNOCKING, I WAITED, LISTENING TO ADAM CORRAL HIS dogs. They seemed excited about company.

"Lie down. I'm not opening the door until you do." Adam's voice was stern, but gentle. "I know you want to see her again. I do too. Please behave."

The knob turned, and I held the pizza box out in front of me. If one lunged my direction, perhaps the food would distract them.

He opened the door. "Hi. You probably heard all that."

"I did. It's cute the way you talk to your dogs."

His brow pinched. "I'm glad you think so. I guess. Can't say I've ever strived for cute."

"Well, you are."

He took the pizza. "Have a seat. I'll grab plates."

The furniture was nice. It wasn't the bachelor pad I'd expected. There was probably a strategy to choosing the right seat on the sofa, but I was pretty sure that no matter where I sat, Adam would sit next to me. I dropped onto the center cushion.

Maybe I used a little bit of strategy.

While Adam hummed in the kitchen, Butch, my kissing buddy, inched toward me, but his belly never left the ground. Sundance clearly felt left out, because after a whine, he did the same.

When Butch reached the couch, he looked up at me with those big brown eyes. Even I could admit he was cute. And I wanted this to work. Determined to give it my best shot, I reached down and patted Butch's head, hoping he wouldn't lick me as a thank you. Looking as happy as a cat with a mouse, that dog jumped up next to me. He rested his head on my leg and closed his eyes.

Sundance nestled against my feet.

Pookie would love me for coming home smelling like dogs.

"I grabbed us Cokes. Oh!" Adam set the plates and drinks down. "Butch, I don't think she wants you there, buddy."

"He's okay."

"Eve, you don't have to have them all over you. I appreciate that you even showed up today."

"I promise to speak up if they bother me."

"All right." He opened the pizza box, and his eyes lit up. "Did my mom tell your mom that I liked black olives on my pepperoni pizza?"

"If she did, Mom didn't tell me. I just ordered it the way I like it. Haley won't let me order it that way. She says it's weird."

"Pineapple is weird. Who's Haley?"

"My friend and temporary roommate. Did you meet her the day the tree fell? She's the one who came and drove me to get my leg looked at."

"Red curly hair?"

"That's Haley." I finished my slice and contemplated a second. "I'm impressed. Butch hasn't tried to steal my food."

"They're good dogs."

"Why'd you get two?" I set my plate aside.

He added another slice to his plate. "I'm gone so much. I didn't want a lonely dog."

I decided not to stop at one slice. While we finished off the pizza, we chatted. Conversation with Adam flowed easily.

I glanced down at the dog still using my leg as a pillow. Would I get used to this? Could I?

"Do y'all rent this place?" I stroked Butch's head.

Adam downed the rest of his Coke. "It belongs to Javi. We've talked about me plenty today. Tell me something about you. Did you always want to work with computers? Were you always a cat person?"

"No and yes. Working with computers pays the bills. I don't hate it, but it's just a job. And I was the girl in middle school with kittens on her folders."

"I'm fighting an uphill battle, huh?"

"But you're fighting. And that counts for something."

CHAPTER 9

"Did you manage to use every dish in this kitchen?" I couldn't even see the bottom of Haley's sink.

She laughed. "I had to make it count. He has *two* dogs. I was more than right."

I turned on the faucet and set to work.

"I'm dying to know what it is about the guy. You swore no dogs. Why is he the exception? And don't talk about his looks. I've seen him, but you care about more than looks." Haley leaned back in her chair and kicked her feet up onto the table.

"He exceeded superhero status before we ever went out. And every time we're together, he's sweet and funny." As I loaded the dishwasher, my mind played through the last week. "Usually the guys I meet are only mildly engaging. After an hour, I find myself glancing at the time. But with Adam, time zips by. I like being around him. I forget about filtering what I say, and he doesn't even seem to mind."

"No filter?"

"It's not gone completely, but because of how we met—the day we don't talk about—there is just more of an understanding. He's heard me ramble, and he still asked me out. I really like him."

"Even if it means being around dogs?"

"For now."

"What did your parents say about moving in?" Haley grabbed a dish towel and dried the pots and pans.

Admitting my delay pricked me with guilt. "I haven't asked yet. I plan to. I just didn't want to talk to Mom earlier because I didn't want her to ask about Adam."

Haley's jaw dropped open. "You haven't told your mom that you're dating Adam?"

"Nope. But he's going to let it drop to his mother that we're going out this Thursday."

"Why the secret?"

"We just didn't want our moms asking questions." I rinsed out the sink. "There. All clean."

"But if your parents move in . . ." Haley wrinkled her nose. "I'm sorry."

"I know. The questions will be endless."

∽

Later that afternoon, when I made it back to the house, Pookie hissed when she sniffed my hand.

"Be nice. Adam puts up with you." I tossed her a treat. Maybe she'd associate that smell with good things. Not that it mattered. I couldn't imagine a scenario where Pookie would meet Butch and Sundance. Well, there was one scenario, but that was so far away from the way things were now.

Before I lost my nerve, I picked up the phone. "Mom, hey."

"I was hoping you'd call. I talked to Mrs. Cardona just a bit ago."

"Oh?"

"Come on, Evelyn. Don't play dumb. She said you were going out with Adam again."

He hadn't waited long after I left to start that game of telephone.

"Yes. We are going out again. He's a real gentleman."

"There is something you should know. I'm only telling you because I don't want you to break that poor man's heart." Mom sounded so serious.

"What, Mom?"

"He has dogs."

My whole family knew about my determination not to date a guy with a dog.

"I'm sure they're nice dogs." I sounded lame.

Mom sighed. "If you really don't want to date a guy with dogs, call him back and cancel. It's not fair to lead him on." She went from all excited about the date to accusing me of leading Adam on.

Was I?

I closed my eyes and pictured Butch snuggled against me. And then I remembered him licking my face. I didn't know what I wanted.

"I'll take it one date at a time, Mom."

"All right. I won't keep you. Just wanted to let you know."

"Okay, well. Oh! I called you to see if you and Dad wanted to stay at my house while the tree damage was being repaired."

"That's sweet of you, dear, but we couldn't invade your space. If things go well with Adam, we wouldn't want to be in the way."

"You wouldn't be in the way."

"I'll mention it to your dad. He'll probably just want to find a short-term rental."

"Mom, I have two extra bedrooms. I don't mind."

"Well, if you insist. We'll do that." She hollered at Dad about the new plan. "When should we move in?"

"Whenever is fine." I padded down the hall and flopped on the bed. "I'll loan y'all my extra key."

"We'll be over in about forty-five minutes. Love you. Bye!"

Forty-five minutes? The hotel was at least twenty minutes away. Had Mom packed in anticipation of me asking? There was no point in worrying about that.

In forty-five minutes, my life would change. I wasn't sure if I was ready.

∼

THIRTY-EIGHT MINUTES LATER, I OPENED THE DOOR.

Mom squealed. "This'll be so fun. Thank you for asking us."

"You'll hardly know we're here." Dad winked.

Pookie ran down the hall, playing with one of her fuzzy toys.

"Your kitty got out of the bedroom." Mom stiffened.

"Pookie lives here, Mom. She doesn't stay in the bedroom all the time." I hadn't even thought about that being a problem.

How was it that Adam was more understanding of my ill-behaved kitten than my mom?

"We'll just have to keep our bedroom door closed." She smiled. "Where should your dad put the bags?"

"In the guest room." I walked out with Dad and helped carry the suitcases. "Oh, here's the spare key. Did y'all hire Derek? He did a great job on my place."

"I did. He'll get started sometime this week." He stopped before walking back into the house. "It'll be about two months. You sure that's okay?"

"Yes, I'm sure."

"We'll try to be good houseguests."

"It'll be fine. I just hope my cat doesn't bother Mom too much."

Dad chuckled as he pushed open the door. "I had a cat when I met your mom."

"What happened to it?" Only part of me wanted to know the answer.

"He scratched her pretty good one night. She sat down and didn't realize he was there. It startled him, and his claws caught her leg as he ran away. We were dating at the time. Mom left and said not to bother calling until the cat was gone."

"That's terrible. What did you do?"

"I gave the cat to Uncle Harvey."

"Muffin was your cat?" I had vivid memories of the orange tabby with the scratchy meow.

"Yep. He lived for a long time. Sweet cat." Dad set the suitcases down. "But I'm sure Mom will get along just fine with your cat."

"I remember Muffin. When we'd visit Uncle Harvey, I'd carry that cat around like a baby. He never scratched me or complained. I loved that cat."

"It's not just that she doesn't like them. She's afraid of them. I doubt she'd ever admit it, but watch her."

"I can't believe you gave away your cat."

"Your mom was worth it."

Suddenly, dots connected in my head, and I propped my hands on my hips. "Why are you telling me this story?"

Dad pulled back in surprise. "We were talking about cats. That's why." His eyes narrowed. "But now I want to know what's got you all fired up."

"Because Mom was giving me a hard time about Adam having dogs."

"If he likes you enough, he'll get rid of them." Dad headed down the hall. "I was going to take your mom out to dinner. You want to come along?"

"Y'all go. I don't much feel like going out. Thank you though."

Dad's words played in my head, and they made my stomach hurt. Adam loved those dogs, and it was clear they loved him. I didn't even want to imagine the sadness in Butch's brown eyes if Adam tried to leave that dog with someone else.

I scooped up Pookie. "Let's get you something yummy. Would you like that?"

She purred as if she knew I was getting her the good stuff.

Mom and Dad left, and I pulled back the foil on a can of pâté while Pookie wove between my legs. I'd only had my little bundle of fur six months, and I couldn't fathom giving her away.

While Pookie licked every last morsel from her dish, I tossed together a quick salad and added smoked salmon. As I drizzled vinaigrette on the top, my phone buzzed.

Do you have houseguests? I need to know so I can gather pebbles to throw at your bedroom window. Adam followed his text with a wink.

They moved in less than an hour after I invited them. So you'll definitely need pebbles.

Any chance I could take you to lunch on Tuesday?

I'd like that. I sent the text then picked up the phone and dialed.

"Hey." Adam's smile added a lilt to his voice. "I'm glad you called."

"Mom and Dad went to dinner. So I have a few minutes of privacy."

"I had fun today."

"Me too." I stabbed at my salad but didn't put any in my mouth.

"I think maybe Butch was once owned by a beautiful brunette."

I wasn't tracking with the jump in the conversation. "Why?"

"He was so excited to see you at the trailhead. He had to be right next to you when you were here at the house. And after you left, he planted himself near the door and was there for hours."

"Are you trying to convince me that your dog misses me?"

"Doesn't it make him more endearing?" Adam laughed. "I'll stop, but I wasn't making it up. He did plop down by the door after you left."

I loved my mom, but I wasn't like her. Offering Adam an ultimatum—me or the dogs—wasn't something I'd ever dream of doing. And while I'd scratched three items off my never list in the last few months, I wouldn't change my mind about that.

Deep down, maybe I was afraid Adam wouldn't choose me. Or maybe it made my heart ache to even think of watching him give up the dogs . . . no matter how big and slobbery they were.

"That's kind of sweet. Maybe I do remind him of someone he used to know."

"He could just have great taste."

"You sure know how to flatter a woman."

"Not all women." His simple phrase set off an explosion in my heart.

I tucked my salad in the fridge and traipsed down the hall. "Did you have pets growing up?"

"When I was little, we had a puppy. I loved that dog. Chocolate was his name. Then we found out my little brother was allergic, and we had to find a new home for Chocolate. After that, we didn't have any pets."

"Oh, Adam. What a sad story. I'm so sorry. Did you ever get to visit Chocolate?"

"No. He went to people we didn't know. I never saw him again. What about you? Any pets growing up?"

"We didn't have any, but my aunt and uncle had this awesome cat. He was the closest thing I had to a pet." I wasn't ready to share the rest of the story.

"I'm glad you found Pookie." This man said all the right things.

"Me too. I'm looking forward to Tuesday." When it came to following the so-called rules of dating, I failed. Playing a game held no interest for me. If I liked him, I saw no reason not to make it obvious. If that changed, I'd be honest about that too.

"Me too." Jingling from his end of the line almost drowned out his words.

"What are you doing? What's all the noise?"

"I'm lying on my back on the floor, tossing two tennis balls across the room. Sometimes instead of fetching, the guys get distracted and start licking my face. That's the jingling sound." He laughed. "I'm sure that sounds absolutely horrid to you."

The licking part did. "I like hearing you laugh."

Flopped across my bed, I talked to Adam for another hour.

CHAPTER 10

Tuesday evening, I walked back into the house, planning to keep quiet about my lunch date.

Mom had only been asking about Adam and our upcoming date every chance she got. She'd asked me about what I planned to wear. She asked if I was planning to get my brows waxed beforehand. And she asked if I was sure I wanted to eat again almost anytime I opened the fridge.

Having them at the house was great.

"I'm home." I scooped up Pookie when she ran up the hall. "Hello, sweetheart. Were you good today?"

Pookie wiggled until I put her down. She followed me into the kitchen and stood beside her food bowl. It had plenty of food, but one little spot of the bottom was visible.

I shook the bowl until food covered the bottom.

Assured that starvation wasn't imminent, Pookie ate.

Mom stood at the stove. "Dinner will be ready in a minute. Why don't you pour yourself a glass of wine? I have some news."

Was I going to need the wine to cope with the news? "Would you like a glass?"

"No. I've already had two." She grabbed a tissue and dabbed at her eyes.

Was it too much to hope that she'd just been cutting onions?

"What's wrong?" Instead of stopping at two fingers, I poured myself half a glass. "Why are you crying?"

"Mandy called me. Mandy Cardona. She's so embarrassed. Please don't be mad at her. She didn't know."

"Didn't know what? Why would I be mad at her?" I pulled in a sip of the sweet white wine. I could go on about fruity high notes, but really, I liked it because it was sweet.

"Adam is dating someone else."

The sweet wine suddenly tasted sour. "What?"

"I can't believe he asked you out again when he's seeing someone."

How did Adam have time to date someone else? Between his work and all the time we spent either seeing each other or on the phone, he had little time to spare.

"What makes you think that?"

Mom lifted chicken out of the pan then added a splash of wine to deglaze. "Mandy called him, but he didn't answer, so she stopped by his house. His roommate answered the door and told her Adam was on a date." She poured the glaze over the chicken and slid a pan of roasted asparagus out of the oven. "On a Tuesday. He must have been dating her awhile if they are getting together in the middle of the week."

It took so much concentration to hold back laughter and not spit my wine. "Let me go change really quick." I needed a few minutes to figure out what to say and to call Adam.

His line was ringing as I closed my bedroom door.

"Hello. How was the rest of your day?" His smooth voice made my heart flutter.

I could play nice or I could spring it on him like Mom had done to me. "You're dating someone else?"

"What? You know that's not true." He didn't even sound rattled, just confused.

I laughed. "Our moms think you are dating someone else. Your mom stopped by while we were at lunch. Javi told her you were out on a date."

"You have to tell your mom the truth."

"I will." I shifted the phone from one side to the other as I pulled off my work clothes. "When she told me, I didn't want to laugh, so I left the room saying I was going to change clothes."

"Is that what you're doing now?"

"Behave. Anyway, when I sit down to dinner, I'll come clean. Just wanted to give you a heads up."

"I appreciate that. Sorry Javi spilled our secret."

"No biggie. I'd love to talk longer, but dinner is already on the table. That is one upside of having them stay here. Mom had dinner ready when I got home."

"Mind if I call you tonight?"

"I'd like that. Talk to you later." I ended the call and ran out to the dining room.

Mom stared at the table, the tissue clutched in her hand, while Dad heaped food on his plate.

I couldn't let the misunderstanding continue any longer. "I was the one at lunch with Adam today." I picked up the tongs to serve myself chicken and asparagus.

"What?" Mom swatted my hand, knocking the tongs free. "Y'all have been sneaking around? His mom and I were so worried. How could you?"

"We weren't sneaking around. We just didn't take out an ad every time we went on a date." I grabbed the tongs again, getting hungrier the longer I sat at the table.

Mom crossed her arms. "How many times have y'all seen each other?"

"Dear, they are adults. She doesn't have to tell us every

time she goes on a date." Dad patted her hand then looked at me. "But if he gives you any trouble, I want to hear about it."

Finally, Mom served herself food. "Now I'm put in the awkward position of having to tell Mandy that her son is keeping things from her."

"I doubt he tells his mom every time he gets a new toothbrush."

Mom was making too big a deal out of it. "You are not a new toothbrush."

"I know, Mom. This chicken is really good. Can I get the recipe?"

"It's just a little of this and that. If I can remember what I put in it, I'll jot it down."

Mom started eating, and I breathed a sigh of relief, thinking the conversation had finally moved on.

"I'm surprised after only a week that you are having lunch together in the middle of a workday."

"He doesn't work a regular schedule. Lunch was a convenient time to see each other."

"What does he do?" Mom cocked her head.

This was where I had to be careful. My parents had no idea that Adam had responded to the call at their house. They also didn't know I was in the bathtub when the tree fell. I'd left out that part of my story. But Mom rarely accepted one-word answers.

I sipped my wine. "He's a fireman."

"Oh? Does he work here in town? What area?" Mom always wanted to know a little bit more.

"Here in town. I'm not sure what station number." That part was true. I had no idea what number was mounted to the side of the station closest to my parents' house.

"Wow. A fireman. Mandy didn't mention that."

Mandy would tell Mom where Adam worked. I'd only delayed the questions. For now, I was okay with that.

Tucked under the covers, I read, waiting for my phone to ring, well buzz. I had the ringer off. Mom didn't need to know about the late-night calls.

Pookie curled up near my feet, tired after chasing her shadow all evening.

When my phone buzzed, I set my book aside. "Hi. If I were a toothbrush, would I be labeled soft, medium, or hard?"

"See, this is why I like you. Medium."

"Why?"

"Well, I sometimes wonder if soft bristles really work well. Are they all fluff and no function? Hard—they're named that for a reason. That's no fun. But you land in that happy medium."

"Good answer." I adjusted my pillows, preparing for a long conversation.

"Did you salvage my reputation?"

"I think so. But apparently my mom didn't know what you did for a living. I told her and she asked about what station—"

"Station 49."

"I told her I didn't know because until just now, I didn't know the number. I haven't told them that I was trapped in the tub or that you rescued me. They think we met on that blind date."

"Maybe it's best if your dad doesn't know about the bathtub part. He might think my intentions are less than honorable."

"Intentions? That sounds so serious."

"I am, Eve."

I sat silently, absorbing his words. I felt the same way, but the dogs were part of the package, and I wasn't yet sure I wanted that. Admitting that made me feel shallow.

"I know. Are you taking the boys for a walk tomorrow?"

"I was planning to take them on a run. I'd love to see you tomorrow since I'm off, but that might be asking too much."

"I could meet all of you at the trailhead again." Spending time with his dogs was the only way I would know if this would work.

"Great. I'd love to talk longer, but my mom is calling. I should probably listen to her lecture now."

"Goodnight. See you tomorrow."

I switched off the light. The next few weeks would be interesting, to say the least. Navigating what felt more and more like a serious relationship with my parents as spectators would be all kinds of fun.

Sensing that I needed a hug, Pookie moved and curled up on my chest.

"I'm worried about whether I can get along with his dogs. What about you?"

Pookie purred.

Maybe I should take a cue from her and not worry. Everything would work out, right?

Maybe.

CHAPTER 11

Adam was already in the parking lot when I pulled in. He jumped out and closed the door.

I stepped out of my car, and he strode up, his brown eyes intense. Without saying a word, he snaked his arms around my waist and backed me against the car. His lips pressed to mine, and I was glad that his arms were holding me up.

When he broke the kiss, he rested his forehead on mine. "I've been wanting to do that since we talked last night."

"Um, wow." I slowed my breathing, hoping my heartrate would follow suit. This was an aerobic exercise I could get used to.

"What I said last night, I meant. I'm not asking you to say anything about how you feel." He glanced at his truck. "I know you have stuff to figure out."

I smoothed the fabric on his t-shirt, appreciating the firm muscles beneath the cotton. "I found out that the cat I loved so much used to belong to my dad. After the cat scratched Mom when they were dating, she told Dad not to bother calling until the cat was gone."

Adam brushed his hand on my cheek. "I'd never ask you to get rid of Pookie."

"I'm glad. But I was thinking of Butch and Sundance. Remember how I said your schedule was part of the fireman package?" I really needed to find a different way of saying that. "Well, those guys"—I pointed at his truck—"they are part of the Adam package. I need to figure out if I can do that."

He swallowed and nodded.

"That's why I wanted you to bring them along." I cupped his face. "I'm trying."

"I know." He pressed a quick kiss to my forehead. "Let's get going." He opened the truck and attached the leashes before the dogs hopped out.

I backed away from the truck.

Butch ran toward me, but the leash stopped him.

"Hey, buddy, stay down, okay?" I inched closer and patted his head.

Adam chuckled. "You might want to be a bit firmer."

Sundance didn't think it was fair that I wasn't giving him attention, so he strained his neck, trying to lick my hand.

"No lick." I used the same voice Mom used when we were driving her crazy. Not that we licked her.

"That's better." Adam clasped my hand, and we started down the trail.

Butch kept trying to walk between us, which made holding hands difficult.

In a spurt of courage, I held out my hand. "Can I walk Butch?"

Adam grinned as he handed over the leash. "Of course."

Butch moved to my other side and trotted along beside me.

"What is it about them you don't like? Besides the licking. I already know that part."

I ducked under a branch hanging over the trail. "I feel like I need a couch before I divulge my deep feelings."

He chuckled.

That was my cue to pour out my heart and soul. "I was at a friend's house, and she had this big dog. Really big. And smelly. He was not well behaved. Anyway, he knocked me over and licked my face. I felt pinned. I couldn't shove him away, and he wouldn't stop."

"Didn't your friend pull him off?"

"She just laughed. I'm sure it looked comical."

Adam stopped walking. "There's nothing funny about that. I'm sorry it happened. And while I can't promise these guys would never do that, I can promise I wouldn't laugh. I'd pull the dog away and help you up."

"Which is why I'm here taking a walk with you and your *big* dogs. You're the reason I'm here."

"Now I want to kiss you again."

~

"How is it possible that you dirtied all these dishes in just three days?" Making good on my lost bet, I loaded Haley's dishwasher and scrubbed pots and pans. Again. "I'm only doing this again because I wanted to be extra nice . . . and because he had *two* dogs."

"I haven't washed a thing since the last time you were here." She laughed. "Tell me about Adam. You have that dreamy look."

"I like him. He's interesting and romantic. And I'm getting to know his dogs, little by little."

"Whoa! You are serious about him, aren't you?"

"We haven't known each other long, but with other guys I've dated—which isn't a long list—after one or two dates, it was clear that the relationship wasn't meant to be. There was no spark. Or it was all sparkles and no substance. With Adam, there are sparks, sparkles, and substance. If I block out the memory of him seeing me shrouded only by leaves and forget he has two dogs, everything seems perfect."

"As long as I've known you, you've avoided dogs. When you came over to my house, you never once touched Comet. And now, when we are out for a walk, you cross to the other side of the trail if someone with a dog is getting anywhere close to us. So, Adam must be some guy." Haley grabbed a pot and dried it with a dish towel.

I'd been terrified of Haley's dog, but never once did I ever tell her. "And everything is a little more complicated because our moms set us up. They are in the middle of it all. We haven't told them about every date. I didn't tell Mom I was meeting Adam tonight."

"But they know about tomorrow."

"Yep. Remember how I told you about his mom thinking he was dating someone else?"

Haley nodded.

"Because of all that, they know we've been seeing each other more than we'd mentioned to them."

"Does he call you every day?"

"He has the last few days because he hasn't been on duty."

"On a scale of one to the best kisser ever, where is he?"

I popped Haley with my dish towel before drying another pan. "Earlier, when I climbed out of my car, he didn't even say hello, he just grabbed me and kissed me. The kind of kiss that makes your knees weak. But that's where his muscular arms come in so handy." My face heated as I remembered both the hello and goodbye kiss. I didn't even tell Haley about the goodbye kiss.

"You need me to splash water on your face? Your cheeks are a bit red."

I stuck my tongue out at her. "Any other questions?"

"Where are y'all going to play kissy face since your parents are at your house, he has a roommate, and the trails close at sundown?"

"I'm sure we'll figure it out."

"Has he been over since they moved in?" Haley pulled a carton of ice cream out of the freezer.

"It's only Wednesday. They moved in on Saturday night." I draped the rag on the counter.

She lifted two bowls out of the cabinet. "Is that a no?"

"He hasn't come over."

"How many times have you seen him since your parents moved in?" She sure asked a lot of questions.

I added an extra scoop of ice cream to my bowl. "Twice."

"Only twice?" She doused her vanilla ice cream with chocolate syrup then held out the bottle.

I took my turn with the chocolate. "We saw each other Saturday. But technically that was before my parents moved in. Adam was on duty Sunday and Monday. Then after he left the station on Tuesday morning we went to lunch. And then today—"

"I get it. Any time he isn't working, he wants to see you."

"Am I crazy, Haley?"

"Yes, but clearly he seems to like that." She stuffed a spoonful of ice cream into her mouth, grinning. "I still can't believe you are dating a guy with dogs. One more never scratched off your list. That's like three in one summer!"

Shaking my head, I took a bite of my ice cream. The next time I added something to my never list, I wasn't going to tell Haley.

CHAPTER 12

I stared at my reflection in the mirror. Counting to ten as I breathed in and out, I glanced at the phone between breaths. Having Adam meet Mom and Dad was unavoidable, and that had my nerves all jittery. I wanted it to go well.

My phone buzzed, and a text popped up. *Pebbles or front door?*

I tapped out a quick reply: *My mom has been pacing for a half hour. She'll be disappointed if I sneak out my window.*

Walking to the door now.

I didn't make it down the hall fast enough. Mom had the door open and was motioning Adam inside as I made it to the entryway.

"I'll let you two say hello, and I'll go get your father." Mom hurried into the other room.

Adam leaned down and gave me a quick peck. "These are for you." A bouquet of vibrant orange roses appeared from behind his back.

"They're gorgeous!"

"I stood in the store for twenty minutes, searching for

what flowers were safe for cats." He bent down and scooped up Pookie. "So if you get into them, you won't get a tummy ache. But there might be thorns, so it's best to stay clear."

Pookie wiggled and meowed.

Behind me, Mom squealed, and Pookie freaked out, scratching Adam's face and arm before he could get her to the floor.

"What beautiful flowers!" Mom seemed oblivious to what had happened with the cat.

I handed the bouquet to her. "Will you put these in water for me? The vases are in the top of the pantry." I grabbed Adam's hand and pulled him down the hall.

Once we stepped into my bedroom, I swung the door closed.

He caught it before it slammed. "I'm okay. Don't be upset."

"I'm getting the bandages."

"Oh joy, kittens again. Not on my face."

I pointed at the bed. "Sit."

His lips quirked into a half grin, and he raised his eyebrows. "I'm guessing your dad is right outside the door by now."

I dabbed at the scratch on his face with a washrag then added antibiotic ointment. "Let me see your hand."

He held it out. "She didn't realize I was holding Pookie. She was excited about the roses."

"I know. I shouldn't blame Mom, and I don't blame Pookie. But every single time you're around my kitten, she hurts you." I smoothed out the bandage. "I feel bad."

Still seated on the bed, Adam pulled me closer. "Pookie and I will figure things out. We just need a little bit of time."

"I love the roses. And I love that you made sure what you brought was safe for her."

"I'm glad you like them." He let his gaze drift down, breaking rule number two. "You look great, by the way."

I took the time to notice his dress shirt and slacks. "So do you."

"Let's go before your parents get the wrong impression." He held my hand as he walked toward the door.

Mom and Dad were seated in the living room, but the television wasn't even on. They couldn't have made waiting any more obvious.

I leaned down to smell the roses. "Thanks, Mom. That vase is perfect for them. The cat got spooked and scratched Adam. Again." I patted his chest. "He was a good sport about it, but I put a bandage on it just to be safe."

He held up his bandaged finger. "It's nice to meet you, Mr. and Mrs. Taylor."

"We've heard so many good things about you." Mom gushed a bit too much.

Dad shook Adam's hand. "Good to meet you."

"You ready?" I tugged on Adam's arm.

Adam nodded toward my parents. "Y'all have a nice evening." When we stepped out the door, he laughed. "In a hurry?"

"They'll be here for two months. I didn't want them to spill all my secrets the first time they met you."

He opened the door for me. "It could be interesting."

"Or horrifying." I buckled my seatbelt as he ran around to his side. "I just think Mom is overly excited because she's afraid I'm never going to meet someone and settle down. If I never marry, she might consider herself a failure. I know she'd consider me a failure."

Adam shook his head. "I don't even know where to start with that."

"It's probably best not to say anything about it. Where are we headed?"

"If it's okay with you, I thought we'd head to the brewhouse. They have a wide variety of options."

"And they have the warm cookie with ice cream on top."

"Then that's where we'll go."

∼

After a fun night, we pulled into the driveway, and I worried about what Mom would do.

Adam hopped out and came around to my side of the truck. He helped me out then pulled me close. "I thought maybe we could have our goodbye kiss here where the view from the windows is blocked by the truck." A chuckle rumbled in his chest.

"I wouldn't put it past my mom to be spying, so I love the idea."

Not two seconds into our goodnight exchange, the front door opened. Dad walked out the front door, carrying a bag of trash. "Oh, hi! I'm just taking out the trash. Don't let me bother you."

I patted Adam's chest. "Well, that didn't go as planned."

"I feel like I'm back in high school." He stepped back and shoved his hands in his pockets.

"How many girls did you kiss in high school?"

His reddened cheeks were visible by the light from the porch. "Not many, but I always felt like I was about to get caught."

"Welcome to my new reality." I trailed a finger down his arm. "I'm sorry you have to deal with this."

"You're worth it."

"You certainly have a way with words. Your shift starts in the morning?"

He nodded. "At seven. Duty ends Sunday morning. So, if you have any time to fit me in, I'd love to see you."

"You have my number."

Adam dropped a quick peck on my cheek. "Your dad is still standing on the porch. I should probably go."

"Bye." I squeezed his hand before walking toward the house. "Hey, Dad."

"Did y'all have fun?" Dad acted like it was perfectly normal to stand on the porch while his adult daughter said goodbye to her date.

"We did." I walked inside and nearly bumped into Mom.

"Adam didn't come in?"

How was I going to do this for two months? "No. He has to be at the station early in the morning."

"Fun fact. He works at the station near our house. I was talking to Mandy tonight. She told me."

Dad flipped the bolt on the door. "Next time he's around, I'll ask him if he was on duty when our tree fell. Maybe he knows about that."

It didn't surprise me that the moms chatted while Adam and I were on a date, but those ladies really needed a new hobby or a more interesting book.

Ready to avoid all conversation, I yawned. "I hope y'all don't mind, but I'm headed to bed. Morning comes early."

"You aren't going to tell us about your date?" Mom put her hands on her hips. "I waited up for you."

"From the looks of things outside, it went well." Dad thought he was funny.

"Adam and I had a nice time. We plan to go out again." Running down the hall would be rude, so I slowly turned. "I like him."

"What about his dogs?" Mom always knew what buttons to push to make something sweet have a sour edge. Probably because she knew me so well. "You hate dogs." Maybe she didn't know me as well as she thought.

Hate was much too strong a word. "I'm sure his dogs are

well behaved." If I didn't exit now, I'd say something that didn't need to be part of the moms' information highway. "Love y'all. Goodnight."

I switched on my bedroom light and called Pookie. She scurried in and climbed up onto my bed. My comforter needed to be replaced thanks to her tiny, sharp claws, but I'd wait to replace it until she was big enough to jump up onto the bed.

While Pookie made herself comfortable on my pillow, I changed out of my dress and pulled on my favorite pajamas. Adam's t-shirt was my favorite thing to sleep in, but that was in a pile of dirty clothes because it desperately needed to be washed.

Pookie cocked her head when a clink sounded at the window.

"What is it, kitty cat?"

The clink sounded again. It sounded almost like hail, except there wasn't any rain. *A pebble!*

I yanked up the blinds. Adam grinned.

The window hadn't been opened in ages, so it took a bit of work to unstick it. But once it was up, I stepped back. "Come on in." I kicked dirty clothes into my closet.

"I never did this in high school." He ducked his head and maneuvered his way inside. "I won't stay long. More than anything I was trying to be funny."

"If my neighbors saw you, it might not be all that funny, but I'm glad you made use of those pebbles." I crossed my arms, suddenly self-conscious. "Just to be clear, when I invited you in, I wasn't inviting you *in*."

His brown eyes twinkled. "Please, explain what you mean."

"You're a smart boy. I think you understand."

"Boy? Ouch."

"I can't believe I'm sneaking guys into my own house to get privacy. Remind me why they are here."

He opened his arms, and like magic, I stepped into them.

"Because a tree fell on their house, and you are a very good daughter."

"Maybe if I go talk to Derek—he's the same guy that worked on my place—he can fast track the repairs."

"Maybe." Adam dropped a kiss on my neck. "Any other ideas?"

"I'm thinking. You can keep doing that." I closed my eyes.

He trailed kisses up my neck, along my jaw, and then his lips found my mouth. I finally got my goodnight kiss.

He broke away and pinched his lips together. "I should go."

"Just like that?"

"Yeah. But I like those kitty pajamas. It's sort of what I expected."

"So you've given thought to what I sleep in?"

"Want to know what I sleep in?" He backed toward the window.

I walked forward, staying close. "Yes, I do."

"A bed." He gave me a quick peck then crawled back out. "Sweet dreams."

I blew him a kiss before closing the window. Then I shot off a text: *It's a good thing this is a one-story. What if my bedroom was on the second floor?*

I'm a fireman. I have a tall ladder.

I climbed into bed. I was no longer trying to figure out if it could work. Now I needed to figure out how to make it work. I was falling in love with Adam and needed to find a way to at least like his dogs.

CHAPTER 13

Since Mom cooked dinner, it seemed only fair that I volunteer to do the dishes. But why did she have to use so many pans? When I made dinner for myself, I typically stuck to one-pan concoctions that were easy to clean up.

I was up to my elbows in soap bubbles when my phone rang. I dried my hands and answered without looking. It had to be Haley. Adam was on duty, and Haley called every night.

"After doing your dishes twice, now, I'm doing a whole mess of dishes at my house. I feel like I'm always doing dishes."

Adam chuckled. "So you're saying that if I volunteer to do them, I can come over any time?"

"Exactly." I managed to get a word out in spite of my shock. "Aren't you at work?"

"I'm at the station. Technically, I'm standing outside. It's easier to talk out here. I hoped to catch you after dinner, but it sounds like you are still doing the dishes. Want me to call back in a bit?"

"No. The dishes can wait. Because what if we are talking later and you get a call? Then I'd lie in bed and worry about who you were rescuing from a bathtub and if they were better looking."

"They wouldn't be."

"You can't know that." I closed my bedroom door and sat on the bed.

"I do know that. Beauty is in the eye of the beholder. That's how I know."

"Did they teach you how to be smooth in fireman school?"

"Yep, but it was an extra-credit course. And another thing, I'm fairly certain that I won't have to rescue a woman from a tub for a while . . . maybe ever. You were a first."

"I didn't expect to hear from you tonight."

"Clearly. I figured that out when you said you'd done my dishes twice. Because you haven't. I'm not complaining, but I feel a little left out. Why are you doing Haley's dishes?"

"Why do you assume it was Haley?"

"Am I wrong?" His smug tone made me wish he was sitting next to me so I could poke him then kiss him.

Saying yes meant that I'd be answering his other question. "Yes, it was Haley. And I did her dishes because I lost a bet."

"About me?" How could he know that?

"You ask a whole lot of questions."

He laughed. "I'll take that as a yes."

"You'll really laugh when you know what the bet was about." Telling him all my secrets might not endear me to him. It definitely didn't fall into the category of coy.

"Now I'm intrigued."

"She bet me that you had a dog."

He was quiet for a minute. "And you wagered that I didn't."

"You hadn't mentioned a dog. But the dog hair on that t-shirt should've convinced me. I was in denial." Footsteps approached my bedroom door, so I slipped into my closet.

Huddled against the far wall, I leaned my head back. "That wasn't a bad thing."

"Sorry about the dog hair. I wasn't even thinking of that when I gave it to you."

"Giving it to me was a sweet thing to do. When I was most vulnerable, you not only saved me from being impaled or crushed by the tree, you saved me from horrible embarrassment. And you were completely professional about it." So much for acting like that day didn't happen.

"While we're breaking rule number one, I want to say that, professional or not, I thought you were cute and funny. Seeing you holding that rose the next night felt like getting a winning scratch-off ticket."

I grinned. "Not the jackpot?"

"I'm still hoping I'll win the jackpot." How dare he say something like that when he was on duty where I couldn't just show up and kiss him!

Or maybe I could. "Do they allow visitors when you're on duty?"

"They do. You going to sneak out your bedroom window?"

"I'm tempted." Flattered and excited, I giggled like a teen. "I'm sitting here, huddled in my closet, smiling from ear to ear."

"Once upon a time, phones were connected to the wall, and you wouldn't have been able to do that. I guess I don't need to ask why you're in your closet."

"I'm pretty sure Mom was hovering outside my door. Don't you just love technology?"

Loud noises sounded in the background. "Duty calls. Gotta go."

"Be safe." I ended the call and stared at my phone. So much for going to visit.

Never before had I thought about Adam being in danger.

But right now, he was jumping into a firetruck to rush to an emergency.

I picked up my phone and called Haley.

Thankfully, she answered right away.

"He called me tonight. But our call was interrupted because the station got a call."

"So he's out doing his fireman thing, huh?" Haley giggled. When I didn't answer, she grew serious. "Oh wow, if I didn't know any better, I'd say someone was close to being smitten."

"We've known each other two weeks."

"And he has dogs. I know all the reasons it shouldn't work, but I also know you're an intelligent twenty-nine-year-old who knows what she wants in a man. I just don't want you rushing into anything."

"You cannot breathe a word of this to anyone."

"Who am I going to tell? My business partner doesn't care—no offense—and other than her, I pretty much only talk to you." Haley sighed. "Remember how I told you about Zach dating the neighbor?"

"Yeah."

"They are standing in the breezeway outside the apartment. She doesn't look happy."

"Are you looking out your peephole?"

"What if I am?"

"I thought you couldn't stand that guy. He's the one who treats you like a kid and calls you Carrot, right? Why do you care?"

"I don't care. It's just—never mind. I'm happy for you. To me, it seems like having him call you from the station is an achievement unlocked."

"It does a little. I didn't expect it."

"I'm going to let you go. With you talking, I can't make out what the argument is about in the hall. Bye."

I stepped out of my closet just as Mom pushed open my bedroom door.

"Why were you in your closet? I thought you were going to do the dishes."

"I'm going to go finish them now." And just like that, I felt sixteen again, and not in a good way.

"And while you're out there, scoop out the cat box. She may be little, but she left a big stink." Mom waved a hand back and forth in front of her nose. "After that, you can come watch a movie with us. I wanted a romance. Your dad wanted an action movie. We settled on a romantic comedy."

"Sounds like Dad lost."

Mom shrugged, grinning. "Do you have popcorn?"

"I'll make some as soon as I finish the dishes." I tucked my phone in my pocket, hoping Adam would text once they got back to the station.

I could pretend like that day in the bathroom never happened, but it was always somewhere in the recesses of my mind. Adam showed his true colors that day. Everything after that was gravy—yummy, delicious gravy.

∽

I STUFFED POPCORN IN MY MOUTH, GLANCING AT MY PHONE between handfuls. The woman in the movie tripped a lot and usually landed in the arms of the same guy every single time.

Never again would I poke fun at those scenes, saying that life never happened that way. Or maybe I should just avoid the word never.

My phone buzzed, and a text popped up on the screen: *Back at the station. Mind if I call late?*

I'd be sad if you didn't.

"Why are you texting? Aren't you watching the movie?" Mom nudged my shoulder.

"I'm watching." I could've made a crack about starring in my own romance, but then Mom would start asking more questions. I didn't want that.

Once the movie was over, I gathered the popcorn bowls. "That was fun."

Mom nudged Dad, who had fallen asleep about ten minutes into the movie. "Thanks for keeping me company, Eve. Maybe next time, Adam can join us."

"I'll ask him. I think he'd like that."

Mom helped Dad up off the couch. "If you're going to be talking to him and texting him day in and day out, it would be nice to get to know him a little." Her jab was anything but subtle.

Was there any question why I battled guilt half the time? "All right. I'll talk to him about it."

"Goodnight." Dad grabbed Mom's hand and tugged her down the hall.

I loaded the rest of the dishes, served myself a bowl of ice cream, and crawled under the covers. Pookie—who had been MIA all evening—climbed up and stared at me.

"I'm not sharing my ice cream with you. But I will give you a treat." I fished kitty treats out of my pocket. "I grabbed a few because I knew you'd eventually come begging."

Pookie purred as she gobbled her treats.

Waiting for my phone call, I read my book and enjoyed a bowl of vanilla ice cream. When I finished eating, I set my dish aside and kept turning pages. Somewhere in the middle of a chapter, I closed my eyes just for a second.

Except it wasn't just for a second.

My phone vibrated, and I slapped the bed, trying to find where I'd laid it down. Pookie's face was buried in my bowl, taking her turn at dish duty.

When I found my phone, I swiped at the screen. "Hello."

"Sorry I woke you."

"I don't mind. Really." I tucked the bookmark in its place and rolled onto my side. "I'll sleep better after talking to you."

"I'll be tucking in for the night soon."

"Mom wants you to come over so they can spend time with you. Maybe dinner and a movie."

"Just say when." Then he hesitated a second. "And I'm sure my parents would like to meet you and put a face to the name."

"I'd love to meet them."

Adam yawned. "I'll let you go back to sleep."

"Thanks for calling. Goodnight." I hugged the phone to my chest.

Just like that, Adam and I moved into a new stage in our relationship. Now, he called me even when he was on duty, and we were planning family dinners.

I sniffed the roses which were now sitting on my side table. "Pookie, if I'm meeting his parents, and he's coming over here to hang out with Mom and Dad, then it probably won't be long before you get to meet the doggies."

Surely somewhere on the internet, I could find a good method for introducing kittens to dogs. I didn't see that going well.

CHAPTER 14

After two weeks of talking every day and a few under-the-radar dates, we scheduled a time for Adam to come over for dinner.

But somehow with my Mom, nothing was ever simple. Instead of a quiet dinner with Adam, she'd asked his parents to join us. I didn't mind that his parents were coming, but I did mind that Mom invited them before mentioning anything to me.

I marked a few more X's on my calendar. It wasn't that I didn't like having Mom and Dad here, but I wanted my house back.

Pebbles hit my window.

After locking my bedroom door, I opened the window. "You came early so we'd have a few minutes to talk?"

"Something like that." He wrangled himself through the small opening. "I'm glad you gave me a heads up about my parents coming. My mom didn't tell me until I was about to walk out the door."

There was no laundry on my floor. I'd even fixed my bed.

He'd snuck through my window enough times that I half expected it when I knew he wasn't working.

"Kiss me. I haven't seen you in days."

He backed me against the wall and did as he was told. There was an extra zing to it. "Who cooked?"

"Mom." I hadn't cooked anything since my mom moved in.

"Do you cook?"

I gave into impulse and toyed with the buttons on his shirt. "You waited until now to ask me that?"

He glanced down at my fingers and quirked an eyebrow. "I cook, so what difference does it make? I was just curious." He grabbed my hand and kissed my fingers. "If your mom cooked, I guess that means we'll be doing the dishes."

"It might be the only time we get alone after walking out of this room."

"I'm not walking out of the room. I'm climbing back out the window and then knocking on the front door." He winked.

"What if tonight doesn't go well?"

"It'll be fine." His pinched brow didn't add much confidence to his statement.

I ran a finger through the crease in his forehead. "And what if it isn't fine?"

"I'll have to find more pebbles."

Cradling his face, I kissed him. "You are amazingly irresistible."

"I think I have a good chance of winning that jackpot."

I wanted to kiss him again, but the doorbell rang. "That must be your parents. Where did you park? Never mind. Tell me later."

He contorted himself to get through the window then leaned in for one last kiss. "See you in a second."

I freshened my lipstick then walked out of my room,

prepared to survive the most embarrassing night of my life. And considering what I'd already lived through, giving it that label wasn't insignificant.

"Hello." I hurried toward the entryway where Mom stood talking with the Cardonas.

A woman who had the same soft brown eyes as Adam smiled. "You must be Evelyn."

"Yes, but everyone calls me Eve."

A man with the same boyish grin walked up with his hand extended. "Meeting you explains a lot. Adam knows how to pick 'em."

At least my parents weren't the only embarrassing ones. In an odd way, that made me feel a little better.

"Come in. I expect Adam will be here soon." I motioned toward the living room.

No one moved.

His mom glanced out the front window. "I'm surprised Adam isn't already here. His truck is parked down the street."

Sheer determination was incapable of preventing a blush. I could feel the heat exploding under my skin. "I hope neither of you are allergic to cats. If so, I can put Pookie in the bedroom for the evening."

"Oh no. We have no trouble with cats." Mr. Cardona tucked an arm around his wife.

Mom leaned close as if she was going to whisper, but she didn't. "Putting Pookie away for the evening would be polite."

"All right." It wasn't a night for arguments. I ran into the kitchen and found my kitty stuffing her face. "Hey, sweetie. I'm going to let you play in the bedroom while we have company."

I hadn't made it two steps out of the kitchen when Adam knocked. At least I hoped it was Adam.

Mom opened the door.

He walked in, holding two small gift bags. "Y'all didn't have to stand here waiting for me." He met my gaze and winked. "I brought something for Pookie."

Seriously. Could this guy be any more amazing?

"Thank you. I was just about to put her in my room for the evening."

He handed me the gift bags and took Pookie. "I'll help."

Somehow, we made it down the hall and to my room without the cat scratching him. And our moms didn't follow. Bonus!

He pointed at the smaller gift bag. "That's for Pookie. The other one is for you."

As soon as I set Pookie's gift on the bed, she buried her face in the tissue.

"It's a little catnip toy." He pulled it out of the bag for her.

Inside my bag was a mug. Emblazoned on the side in red letters was one simple sentence: *I love you*.

I stared at the mug.

"I saw that you had a collection, and I thought one more might be good." He leaned down to meet my gaze.

"It's my new favorite." I leaned my head on his chest, overcome with emotion.

He wrapped his arms around me. "I love you, Eve. I don't care if tonight goes horribly. It won't change the way I feel."

"I love you too."

As soon as the words left my lips, his were touching mine, and for a second, all the world was perfect.

"Jackpot." His brown eyes twinkled.

I inched up on my toes and snaked an arm around his neck, pulling him to my lips again. "They are going to wonder why we're taking so long."

"True. We should probably go back out there. But I wanted to tell you before dinner. My parents—my mom—

will likely bring up my ex. It's not because I talk about her or because I'm harboring feelings."

"You're just warning me that your mom wants you to get back together with your ex, is that it?"

"Maybe." He crinkled his nose. "But I don't share her sentiment."

"We'll talk more later. I can't believe you planned to give this to me in front of everyone." I started toward the door.

He caught my arm. "Following you down the hall wasn't an accident. Did you notice that I didn't say anything about a gift for you? I wouldn't make things awkward on purpose."

My gaze swept over him, taking in the man who held my heart. "What's better than best?"

"I'm not sure there is a better than best. By definition, it's the *best*." The dimples appeared.

"Well, we have to figure out something because you just moved up a tier. And prior to all this, you were at best."

Grinning, he opened the bedroom door. "Bestest?"

"That'll work for now. But if we put our heads together, I think we can come up with something better."

"If *putting our heads together* means kissing, I'm on board with that."

I glanced down the hall to make sure we were still alone. After one more kiss, I patted his chest. "Stop kissing me. We need to go have dinner."

He grinned.

Thankfully, Pookie didn't even try to run out. She was rolling around on the bed with her catnip-filled fish, acting happy as a clam.

Hand in hand, Adam and I walked down the hall and into the dining room. Everyone was already seated at the table.

Mom jumped up. "Eve, will you help me in the kitchen?"

Lecture time.

"Sure." After Adam squeezed my hand, I followed her into the kitchen. "What do you need me to do?"

"Dear, you really want to make a good impression. It's important that his parents like you. What are they supposed to think when the two of you go off to your bedroom?"

Silly me, I thought the really important part was Adam liking me. "We were talking." And kissing, but I wasn't about to say that. "Do you need my help?"

She handed me a basket and pulled a tray of rolls out of the oven. "Put those in the basket. I'll carry in the casserole."

Dinner was off to a great start. If I kept my thoughts on the mug sitting in my bedroom, I could make it through the evening with my sanity intact. I set the rolls on the table and sat down next to Adam.

Pale, he offered a weak smile and clasped my hand under the table.

His mom looked up and met my gaze, "I was just telling them about why I hatched the plan to set Adam up. After he broke up with Lilianna—she was such a sweet girl—anyway, after that, we worried about him. I don't think he went on a single date for over a year. But clearly, he doesn't tell me about every date."

Adam's hand tightened around mine.

"But when your mom and I started talking, we knew what to do." She turned to face Adam. "Did you know that Lilianna got a new puppy? She dropped by the other day to let us see him. So cute. We'll be pet sitting for her at the end of the month, so we wanted to spend a little time with the new puppy."

Clearly his mom was a dog-lover. *Fabulous*.

"What kind of dog?" I served myself food one-handed, hoping no one would notice.

"Honestly, I've never seen a dog so cute. She bought a

Chipoo, a cross between a pure-bred Chihuahua and a pure-bred Poodle."

"I bet that is a cute combination." Mom beamed.

When Adam was the only one not eating, I shot him a look. He let his fingers slip off my hand then picked up the serving spoon. "Mrs. Taylor, dinner looks amazing. Eve tells me you've been a big help by cooking most nights."

"It's the least I can do. She's been so generous to let us stay here."

"She is pretty awesome." He moved his roll away from the rest of his food.

Dad pointed his fork at Adam. "I meant to ask you—I think your station is the one that showed up when the tree fell. We weren't home. Only Eve was there, but I wasn't sure if you'd heard about it."

"I did. That was unfortunate. How long will the repairs take?"

"The damage was significant, but our contractor said he'll be done in three weeks. He's worked really hard to get it done ahead of schedule." Dad added butter to a roll. "I'm sure Eve will be glad to get her house back. Then the two of you won't have to stand in the driveway after your dates."

I was near maximum embarrassment, and we weren't even to dessert yet.

Dinner continued, and nothing more was said that made me want to crawl under the table.

"Let me grab dessert." Mom jumped up, her smile wide.

As she carried her cheesecake to the table, the thought popped in my head that we were in the clear. I waved the thought away, not wanting to tempt fate, but it was too late. Just thinking it had given a challenge to the universe. For the second time this summer, dying from embarrassment seemed possible. And I didn't even know what was coming.

"Usually I add a blackberry swirl to my cheesecake and

top the whole thing with fresh blackberries, but Eve said I should just make it plain. I don't know why. But here it is—plain. I made a blackberry topping and a strawberry topping for those of us who like our cheesecake a bit fancier." Mom set the dessert on the table then ran back to the kitchen.

Adam leaned close. "You noticed and remembered."

"I did." It probably wasn't the best idea to tell him it worried me at the time.

Mrs. Cardona laughed. "Adam doesn't like his cheesecake with anything in it or on it. He also eats his pasta plain and his salads without dressing. He is the pickiest of all the kids."

"I'm surprised he ate the casserole." Mr. Cardona stirred cream into his coffee. "Normally, he doesn't like his foods to touch."

Besides eating plain cheesecake and keeping things separate, Adam hadn't been too weird about his food. All the cracks about his pickiness seemed undeserved.

Listening to them poking fun at him made me want to jump to his rescue. "When I was younger, I couldn't stand oranges. Now I eat them all the time. The little mandarins are my favorite." My addition to the conversation drew blank stares from all four of the parental units.

"Those clementines are good too." Adam ate a bite of cheesecake. "Wow. This is really good. Creamy."

"Thank you." Mom doused her slice with the blackberry topping.

Inspired by Adam's mention of another type of citrus, I had an idea. "Cara Cara oranges are tasty. Have you had those?"

Would Adam catch on to my silly little game? Haley and I had done it during high school more than once. We'd pick a topic and see how many mentions or variations we could drop before people figured out what we were doing. It kept the conversation interesting.

He didn't disappoint. "I haven't tried those. I think they are usually right next to the Mineola tangelos, aren't they?"

Dad sipped his coffee. "When I was young, they didn't have all these fancy choices. We were lucky to get navel oranges."

Now my dad was in on the game. I'm not sure he knew that though.

"I remember having those oranges that were dark red inside. What are those called?" Mr. Cardona's brow pinched as he tried to remember.

"Blood oranges." Adam tapped the table. "Oh, and I like tangerines."

I heaped a little extra strawberry topping on my slice of cheesecake. "Mom, this is berry good."

She rolled her eyes. "Very punny."

"Orange you glad I didn't say the name of a citrus fruit?" I giggled at my own stupid joke. Living with my parents had reduced me to behaving like a child.

Adam coughed to cover his laugh.

"How are the strawberries, dear?" Mom gave me one of her scolding looks while using her sweetest voice.

"Delicious." They were so good in fact, I preferred to use my mouth to eat rather than talk about how tasty they were.

Mom tapped the edge of the bowl. "They are from a farm in Poteet."

Mrs. Cardona beamed. "I grew up in Poteet on a strawberry farm."

"I lived in the same area. Did you grow up in Poteet also?" Mom pushed her dessert plate away and narrowed her eyes like she was trying to access the files stored in the back of her brain.

Mr. Cardona nodded. "Near there."

"You seem so familiar. Even the last name is familiar, but I can't place you. Where did you go to school?"

"Maybe you saw me on the football field. I was the star quarterback." He grinned.

Mom jumped up and excused herself. If I had to guess, Mr. Cardona looked nothing like he did in high school. Okay, maybe he did a little . . . just enough to be familiar but not recognizable.

Dad followed her to the doorway. "You okay?"

"Yes. I'll be right back." She tapped his cheek.

He seemed convinced she was all right. I wasn't. The evening had just gotten weird.

Adam stood. "Let me help you clear the table. Then I'll do dishes."

"Thanks." I gathered plates and followed him into the kitchen. When we were out of earshot of everyone else, I slipped my arms around his waist. "I'm glad we talked earlier. I'm not sure this is what I imagined when you said that it would be fine."

He kissed my forehead. "I didn't know my dad dated your mom. I'm guessing that's what sent her running out of the room."

"Maybe. This might make get-togethers a bit awkward."

"I vote we skip get-togethers for a while. The embarrassment from tonight should last me months, maybe even a year." He began rinsing and loading dishes. Anything that couldn't go into the dishwasher, he washed then handed to me to dry.

"You didn't complain about the pizza." I dried the dishes then put them away.

"I'm also not five anymore." He splashed water at me. "I've learned something this past month."

"Please, tell me."

"Life with you isn't dull. Ever." He faked a wince when I poked him in the side.

"Before the lightning storm, my life was very boring. Even after that, it wasn't all that exciting until the tree fell."

"So I rescued you from boring?" He turned off the water and shifted to face me.

"You did."

Inching closer, he lowered his voice. "You want to come over later? Javi is out of town again."

It had been a week since I'd been around the dogs. My inclination when they ran toward me was to back away, but I was trying. "Sure."

"Great. We'll share a giant bowl of popcorn and watch something funny."

"Orange you glad I didn't say no?"

His hands still wet, he picked me up. "So berry glad."

Not liking his dogs would be a horrible reason to lose Adam.

I FOLLOWED ADAM TO HIS FRONT DOOR, GIVING MYSELF A silent pep talk. *Be firm. They are nice dogs. He's worth it.*

He pushed open the door and told Butch and Sundance to sit. They obeyed but had perfected the art of dancing while still technically sitting.

I didn't avoid them. Patting their heads, I kept my face away from theirs. "Hey, guys. We're going to watch a movie. You want to watch it with us?"

Adam chuckled. "I'll make popcorn." He walked into the kitchen, and Sundance followed.

Butch stayed in place, staring at me.

Adam called out from the other room, "He likes you."

"He's sweet." I dropped onto the sofa and patted the seat beside me.

Butch jumped up and curled up almost in my lap.

I was maybe starting to like having him do that. "You can't steal my popcorn. I don't share popcorn."

"Uh-oh. Should I make two batches?"

"I'll share with you. This time." I kicked my shoes off. "I'm glad the evening ended okay. I was kind of worried for a little bit."

"Yeah, hearing the story of how your mom flirted with my dad, only to realize he was interested in her friend was funny." He sat down and handed me the bowl. "Funny, scary, or romantic?"

"Funny."

After clicking play, he draped his arm around me. This wasn't bad. The dogs hadn't licked me. Our parents didn't hate each other. And Adam loved me.

Life was good.

CHAPTER 15

*M*om and Dad were as excited about the completed repairs as I was about getting my house back. Instead of two months, it had only taken seven weeks to get the house move-in ready. Seven weeks and two days—not that I was counting. Okay, I was.

"I can't wait to see how y'all redid the bathroom." I glanced back at Adam as I followed Mom down the hall. "It's sweet of you to come help move furniture back into place."

"I'm trying to impress them." He quirked an eyebrow, and his expression made me wish we were alone at my house.

"It's working." I'd tell him later how Mom gushed about him every chance she got.

Mom motioned like Vanna White at the bathroom door. "Go in and see it."

When I walked in, I wasn't expecting her to practically push Adam in behind me. So much in the bathroom had changed . . . except the tub. That looked exactly the same.

Flashes of the tree and the embarrassing horror flooded back. Heat rose in my cheeks, and I avoided looking at the tub. If I acted weird, Mom would know something was off, or she'd at least start asking questions. And I wanted to keep what happened a secret as long as possible.

Then Adam stepped closer to make room for Mom and Dad to enter the bathroom, and claustrophobia set in.

I needed to get out of the bathroom. I turned, which landed my face in Adam's chest. That did not make this easier.

To his credit, he stuck his hands in his pockets. "This looks great. Don't you think, Eve?"

"Yes, I love the new paint color. Pink is a great color in here." It wasn't what I would've chosen, but it worked in that room. "And the new sink is awesome." Faking normal seemed to be working.

Mom beamed. "I wanted to put in a whole new tub, but it was faster and cheaper to have the tub refinished and repair the few broken tiles."

I was glad they opted for the faster and cheaper.

"So now you can tell the other guys at the station how things turned out. Weren't they the ones that came out?" Dad patted Adam on the back.

"Our station responded. I'll let them know. It's nice to hear good news after the fact." Adam glanced at the door.

Faking it wasn't working anymore. I needed out of that tiny space. It was embarrassing enough being in here with Adam again. At least I was wearing more this time. And the room wasn't made for four people. But standing there, I felt trapped all over again.

Adam slid one hand out of his pocket and pressed it to the small of my back. "Eve said they redid the back patio also. Is that right?"

"Yes. I'll show you." Mom pushed on Dad. "You have to go so we can get out. You're blocking the door."

"Oh. I guess I am. Sorry about that."

Adam gripped my hand. "Lead the way." His gentle encouragement steered Dad back on track.

Having Adam touch me did not invoke the horror and penetrating embarrassment I expected. Instead, it was comforting.

When we stepped outside, I inhaled as if outside air was the antidote to my discomfort.

Adam slipped an arm around my waist and glanced down at me with eyebrows raised.

I smiled up at him. "I'm okay."

Dogs and all, this guy was a catch, and I'd almost let my embarrassment get in the way. Today, he'd helped me keep the details of the rescue a secret, but I knew that when I least expected it or at the most inopportune time, my parents would find out.

"This patio is great, Mr. Taylor. Looks like the perfect place to grill steaks or smoke a brisket."

Dad grinned. "My thoughts exactly. Let us know when you're free, and we'll plan something."

"I'd love that." Adam was using the L word more often lately.

I'd noticed.

∼

When we were finally alone at my house, I handed Adam a glass of water and the bowl of popcorn. "Water with ice. And popcorn. I'm ready."

"Before we start the movie, do you want to break rule one?" He'd waited until now to bring it up.

Probably because I hadn't brought it up on the drive home.

"I'm really okay. It was just—I couldn't stay in there."

"Feeling trapped is completely normal. If you were

embarrassed, you don't need to be." He flashed a smile. "I hardly remember a thing."

"I'm not sure that calling me forgettable is going to make me feel better."

He paled. "I only meant—"

I kissed him. "You could see through those branches, huh?"

"A little." He blew out a breath. "Ready to watch the movie?"

"Are we done talking about it?"

"We've wandered into dangerous territory. Best to obey the rules, I think."

I leaned my head on his shoulder. "That's why I love you."

"The only reason?"

"One of them."

Instead of clicking play, he took the glass out of my hand then trailed a finger along my jaw before cupping my face in his hand. Our lips met, and I wrapped my arms around his neck.

Adam hugged me closer, never separating our lips, and leaned back against the end of the sofa.

His mouth moved against mine. Clinking on the table interrupted the moment. Adam broke the kiss and sighed.

Pookie dipped her paw in his glass then licked off the water.

"Your precious little kitten does whatever she wants, doesn't she?" He sounded almost irritated.

"Pookie, quit!" I jumped up and grabbed the glass. "I'll get you a new one."

Why did his question irritate me so much? It wasn't so much the question itself but the way he'd worded it that bothered me.

I tucked his glass in the dishwasher and grabbed a clean

one. I was back in the living room in no time flat. "Here, water with ice again. I'm sorry. But at least she didn't—"

Adam rubbed his hand. "If you were going to say scratch me, she did that while you were in the kitchen. I'm not her favorite person."

"Should I get the bandages?"

"No. I go on duty in the morning. The last time I forgot and showed up with a kitten bandage. The guys had a field day." He crossed his arms.

I set the water on the table. "Do you still want to watch the movie?"

"Why wouldn't I?" He snapped the question.

"Maybe because you're being as moody as a cat." I scooped up Pookie and sat on the opposite end of the sofa.

Laughter wasn't what I expected as a response.

With his arms still across his chest, Adam tossed his head back and filled the house with a deep robust laugh.

Had I missed something? "What? Why are you laughing?"

"Pookie isn't the only one with claws, I see." He held out his hand.

"You accuse me of having claws, and now you want to hold my hand?" I was only mildly successful at keeping the irritation out of my voice.

"May I hold Pookie?"

"Are you sure you're brave enough to try again?" I handed over my precious kitten.

She didn't seem happy about it because she wriggled in his hand, her claws outstretched.

If he was afraid, he didn't let it show. "Darlin', running into burning buildings is less scary than dealing with your cat, but she's part of the package, as they say." He held Pookie up in front of his face. The man was brave. "We need to figure this out. I'll be around a lot, and I'm not a big fan of kitten bandages. I like your human. Please stop trying to take my hand off."

Kitty gave a little whine.

"Is that a yes?" He kissed the top of her head. "I'll pretend it is."

As soon as he put her down, she scurried away.

I felt a bit swoony after watching him have a heart-to-heart with Pookie.

"I think it will take treats to win her over." He inched closer. "What will it take for you?"

"You don't like her, do you?"

"She's growing on me. It's probably from the little bits of DNA she leaves under my skin." He could be adorable and frustrating at the same time. "Now back to my other question." He scooted even closer. "Will you forgive me?"

"I want you to like my cat."

"Do you like my dogs?" He raised an eyebrow.

"I do. I mean . . . at first, I didn't. I hate saying that out loud. They are big and slobbery. But the more time I spend with them, the more I grow to like them."

He closed the small gap. "I'm really glad to hear that."

"Just don't tell Haley!" I snuggled next to him. "Now start the movie."

"Yes, ma'am." He kissed me on the top of the head.

Was he going to bring me treats too?

CHAPTER 16

Weighed down with grocery bags, I dropped a freshly chiseled key onto the entry table. I still hadn't managed to get my spare key back from my parents.

Haley had been hounding me about planning a girls' getaway weekend, and I'd decided that if Adam would look in on Pookie to make sure she had food and water, then a weekend away would work.

All that was left to do was ask Adam. He showed up with treats every time he came over, and Pookie ran up to him when she heard his voice. It seemed like things were better with that situation. Mostly. She had scratched him a few more times.

And that was why I'd planned a special dinner. Buttering him up with a home-cooked meal wasn't a bad thing, right?

Besides, it wasn't like I never cooked, but for this dinner, I was going all out.

I dropped the bags on the table and shook my hands, trying to get the blood back into my fingers. That was the price of getting everything inside in only one trip.

The phone rang as I emptied bags. "Hey, what's up, Haley?"

"Have you decided?" She had a one-track mind.

I set the steaks next to the stove. "If Adam will watch Pookie for me, then we can go. I'm going to ask him about it tonight. So wish me luck."

"You'll need it after all the times your cat has torn him up. Are you still making her catch her treats? Are you using sign language with her?"

"I sometimes make her catch the treats. Adam was impressed by that little trick, but I don't know sign language."

"I only know a few signs. You have access to the internet, don't you?" Haley laughed.

"How are you? Why the urgency to get away?"

"Work has been stressful, but the new client that's been taking up my whole life will have everything she needs by the end of the week." She sighed. "Oh! Did I tell you about my neighbor breaking off the engagement?"

"When you were spying through the peephole?" I could totally picture her standing on the mini stepstool, watching everything.

"Do you want to know what it was about or not?"

"Tell me about Zach, the guy you don't care about." Back and forth across the kitchen, I put groceries away and laid out items that I'd need for dinner.

"I like people watching, and, besides that, he's my brother's best friend. Hank might want to know if Zach is going through a rough spot."

Adding as much sap to my voice as I could muster, I said, "You're such a good sister and friend."

"Whatever. Anyway, she was mad—hollering in the breezeway mad—because he missed their special dinner."

"He stood her up?"

"He called her to say his friend needed him. You know who that was? Hank. He skipped dinner to hang with Hank the day he was served with divorce papers." Haley's voice cracked. "There was part of the argument I couldn't hear. But he even called her ahead of time to let her know. She didn't care. Ranting about how he put his friend first, she ended up sobbing so much she couldn't talk."

"What did he do?"

"I almost felt sorry for him. He looked like he might be sick." The sympathy in her voice was unmistakable.

What kind of friend would I be if I didn't push at least a little? "Almost?"

"I felt *so* bad for him. Imagine being tormented for being a great friend. Isn't that awful? It wasn't like he snuck away to go camping."

"That's random."

"Hank and Zach like to go camping. They've done it since high school."

"Did they know you were listening?"

Her long pause answered the question. "Maybe. He looked right at the peephole once or twice."

"Busted."

"But he doesn't know I live here." Haley had a slight panic in her tone, which was quite unusual. "Eventually, she slammed the door, and he left."

"How do you know she ended the engagement?"

"Because right before he walked away, she opened the door again and threw the ring at him. I didn't know what she'd thrown until he picked it up, but how sad is that?"

"Is that when he looked at you?"

"Yes, but I think that was because I gasped. He totally heard me."

"Poor guy. I'd love to chat longer, but Adam will be here in just a little bit, and I want to have the steaks ready."

"Steaks? Yum. He'll totally say yes to taking care of Pookie."

"I hope so. Bye." I tossed my phone aside and set to work.

Thirty minutes later, I was staring at the clock, hoping Adam would show up before the steaks were ready. He'd never been more than seven minutes late. Tonight was not when I wanted that to change.

Two minutes early, he knocked.

I ran to the door, wiping bits of food off my apron. "Hi."

His gaze swept over me. "You look rather domestic tonight. And what smells so amazing?"

"Dinner. Let's talk in the kitchen. I don't want the zucchini to burn."

"Be right there. Coming up the walk, I realized I had mud on my shoes." He kicked off his sneakers and followed me into the kitchen. "You really went all out tonight. Steaks?"

Honesty was the best policy, right? "I have a favor to ask, so I made something special."

He eased up behind me and brushed my hair over one shoulder.

I stirred the veggies, loving the feel of his arms around me.

Dropping kisses on my neck, he whispered, "You can ask favors without making me steak."

"It's kind of a big favor."

"Let me guess. You want to rearrange furniture. Is that it?"

"No. But do you think I should? I've never had the couch against the other wall." Teasing him was too much fun.

"We can talk about how to rearrange furniture later. Tell me about this favor."

"You aren't even going to enjoy a delicious steak first?" I plated the food.

He took the plates and carried them to the table. "You're stalling."

"I haven't kissed you." I leaned close.

He stayed an inch away. "Now, I'm starting to worry."

I gave him a quick kiss. Cold steaks would not help my case. "Take one bite, and then I'll ask."

Grinning he dropped into a chair after pulling mine out for me. "Does it involve a risk of death?"

"Only maiming." I flashed my best smile.

He shot me a side glance as he cut into his steak. One bite disappeared into his mouth, and I waited, watching his expression.

When he finished chewing, he cut off a second piece. "Wow. So good." Had he forgotten about the favor? After another bite, he glanced at me. "You can ask any time."

The best way to ask was just to let the words tumble out. "Haley wants me to go away with her on a girls' weekend. I was hoping you'd check in on Pookie while I was gone."

He grinned again. "No problem. I can do that. The way you were acting, I thought it would be something hard or terrible."

"Like what?"

"I refuse to answer that question. It could definitely get me into trouble."

"I bought new bandages."

He narrowed his eyes. "More kittens?"

"Puppies. I thought you'd like those better."

He shook his head but didn't respond. The steak had his full attention. He didn't even seem to notice Pookie sitting at his feet.

∼

Adam flopped onto the sofa and rubbed his belly. "Thank you. I had no idea you could cook like that."

Pookie jumped up into his lap.

"Sorry, little one, I was distracted by food. I forgot to give you treats." He yanked a small plastic bag out of his back pocket and shook a few into his hand. "Here you go."

She gently took them out of his hand one by one, purring the entire time.

Once the treats had all been gobbled up, he gave her a good scratch, and then after a quick meow, she jumped down and waddled off.

"I think she likes me." He seemed pleased.

"She'd be silly not to." I settled next to him. "You really don't mind taking care of her? I'd probably leave midday on a Friday and be back late on a Sunday."

"You just need to schedule it on a weekend when I'm not on duty, but I don't mind at all."

I jumped up and ran to the entry table. When I got back to the couch, I snuggled in beside him and held out the black key that was painted to look like a cat. "You'll need this to get in the house. I really appreciate it."

"A cat key. How cute." After tucking the key in his pocket, he brushed a finger along my cheek. "Just let me know when."

He pulled me to his lips, and I was again reminded of how nice it was to have my house back.

Meowing interrupted us. Pookie stood on the sofa next to me with part of a shoelace hanging out of her mouth.

"Oh no, kitty. Which of my shoes did you chew on?" I wasn't sure if Pookie was rotten or bored.

Adam groaned. "I think it's from my shoes. I kicked them off by the front door."

"I'll buy you new laces." I pushed up off the sofa. "There are still places open."

He clasped my hand and tugged me into his lap. "Don't worry about it right now. I'd rather continue what we were doing."

"If you're sure."

"Absolutely positively sure." He grinned. "This is even better than dinner."

"I made dessert. It's chilling in the fridge."

"We'll have plenty of time for that." He chuckled as Pookie rubbed her face on his feet. "I think maybe she's jealous. You notice she almost always shows up when I kiss you."

"I've noticed."

Watching the cat out of the corner of his eye, Adam leaned in and kissed me, just a quick peck. Pookie jumped onto his leg. He kissed me again, and that little cat put her paws on his chest and bumped her nose against his chin.

He chuckled. "I think she likes me better."

"Because she knows you have treats in your pocket."

He reached into his front pocket. "I brought you something too." He held out a small box.

Adam had been all kinds of romantic since that first blind date when he showed up with the bouquet of yellow roses. Surely the box he'd just handed me didn't contain a ring. It was about the right size, but lounging on the sofa wasn't where I expected him to propose. Not that I'd say no. I didn't need a grand gesture, but I wanted to know it wasn't an afterthought.

"I'm guessing that little box doesn't contain kitty treats." I smiled, feeling a bit foolish for even thinking he'd propose. We were serious, but were we that serious?

"Are you going to stare at it or open it?" He nudged me with his elbow.

I lifted the lid off the tiny cardboard box then swatted his arm. "Adam Cardona!"

He chuckled. "It's been three months since that day, so I wanted to get you something special."

"Even though it totally breaks rule one, I love it." I lifted the necklace out of the box, and the bubble bath pendant dangled in the middle. "The little person even has long hair."

"I tried to find one with her hair up, but this was the best I could do."

Letting my mouth hang open wasn't a great look, I'm sure, but having him remember that detail stunned me. "You remember that?"

"Vividly."

If I wasn't sure the heat flooding my face was noticeable, he made it clear when he brushed my cheek. "And I remember your blush."

I swallowed, feeling nearly as vulnerable as I did that day in the tub.

"When I touched the scratches on your face, your reaction made me wish I'd met you under different circumstances."

"And then you did."

That wide smile cut across his face. "I did indeed." He trailed his thumb across my lips. "I have an idea."

If the idea involved kissing me, I was all for the plan. "I'm listening." At that moment, he could've suggested we hike in Big Bend during the hottest part of August and I might've agreed.

He leaned in closer, his thumb still moving back and forth. "Since we are getting along swimmingly—I mean, I'd say we are. Do you agree?"

I nodded.

He slid his hand into my hair and danced his lips on mine.

If I was being buttered up before he asked the question, it was working. And working well. Maybe his parents wanted to have dinner again.

"What if we introduce Pookie to the boys?"

Saying no wasn't an option. I knew that. But in spite of being buttered up, I hesitated. "She's so little, and they're so big."

"They won't eat her."

"I know they won't. We should do that. I mean, we want them to get along, right?"

"I do." His brown eyes twinkled with his not-so-subtle answer.

"Okay. I'll read up on the best way to do it."

"I can bring the boys here so Pookie is on her own turf. She'll have lots of places to hide." He squeezed my hand. It almost sounded like he'd already done some research. "I wasn't sure you'd say yes."

"I really hope they don't hate each other."

"You and me both."

CHAPTER 17

All the research in the world wasn't going to make the meet and greet for our beloved pets any easier. We just had to get Pookie, Butch, and Sundance together.

I stood at the front window, watching for the truck. Pookie was in my bedroom, and she wasn't pleased about having her freedom limited. She meowed over and over.

"Kitty, trust me. You'll want to be in there. I'll let you out in a bit."

Adam pulled in the driveway, and I sucked in a deep breath. I was more nervous about my cat meeting his dogs than I'd been about meeting Butch and Sundance myself. Waiting on the front porch, I watched him as he lifted two dog beds out of the back, and then with one bed in each hand, he carried them toward the house. The way it made his biceps bulge was not at all unattractive.

He walked up to the door, and I smiled, still admiring his toned and tanned arms.

"Um . . . are you going to open the door?"

"Oh, sorry. I got distracted." I pushed open the front door

and moved aside. "The beds are the safe place for Butch and Sundance?"

He nodded as he dropped them down in the living room. "Yes. Is Pookie in your room?"

"Locked up and not happy about it."

He turned then stopped. "Hey, if this first time doesn't go well, don't be discouraged, okay?"

"All right." I could at least pretend not to be discouraged.

But the fact that he'd even said something like that meant that he worried it wouldn't go well. And that nugget of truth only added to my worry.

"Bring them in. This waiting is making me crazy."

"Sure. But first—" He caught my mouth with his. Passionate, he danced his lips on mine. As they tangoed, I leaned in closer. In moments like these, I appreciated his muscles even more. His arm was pretty much the only reason I was still on my feet and not puddled on the floor.

"Now I'll go get the boys."

I followed him out to the truck. The way Butch got all excited when he saw me was endearing. He didn't seem to notice that his size made me nervous. Anytime we were in the same space, he wanted to be right next to me.

Adam handed me Butch's leash.

"Hey there. You are being a good boy. Are you ready to meet the kitty?"

With ears perked up, Butch cocked his head as if he understood.

Sundance ran circles around Adam who was now tangled in the leash.

"He loves to go to new places, if you can't tell." Adam freed himself then led the dogs into the house and straight to the living room.

Pookie must have sensed intruders because she'd gotten uncharacteristically quiet.

Adam unhooked the leashes. "You boys be nice. This is Eve's place. Give it a sniff, then we'll let you meet the resident cat."

Sundance barked at the last word.

"That's probably not the best way to make friends, buddy." Adam patted both dogs.

Butch padded over to me and sat, looking up with those big brown eyes. After getting a little love, he nosed around the living room, sniffing everything.

Sundance followed Butch around for a few minutes, but when Pookie meowed, he stopped. His ears perked up, and he took off down the hall.

Butch followed but with more caution.

Adam and I stayed a few feet back, watching the whole time.

Sundance sniffed at the door, trying as hard as he could to get his nose underneath.

Butch stared at the door then looked back at Adam. For such a big dog, Butch was timid. Sundance, on the other hand, wanted to meet a new friend.

After letting them sniff a bit, Adam called the boys back to the living room.

"I picked up a few toys for them." I laid the rope and squeaky toys on the ottoman.

Adam stretched out on the floor and played tug of war with Sundance while petting Butch. "Have you and Haley planned your trip?"

"Weekend after next . . . if that still works for you." I sat down on the floor beside Butch.

"I've marked it on my calendar. Where are y'all headed?"

"Oh, you want to know about what we're going to do!"

"Right. In the manual, it says that a boyfriend should show interest in their girlfriend's life." He glanced at me out of the corner of his eye.

I loved that mischievous streak. "Fredericksburg. That's where we are planning to go. Haley found this house to rent for the weekend."

"Do you cook or eat out when you go away on weekends?"

"We stuff ourselves at a restaurant at lunch or dinner. But we take plenty of snacks to sustain us the rest of the time."

"And what do y'all do when you aren't eating at a restaurant?"

"Talk, laugh, watch romantic movies, paint our toenails. Stuff like that."

"You going to talk about me?" His grin begged for a kiss.

I obliged. "Probably a bit. But I try not to go on and on because Haley doesn't have what I have."

"You don't want her to feel bad because you have such an awesome boyfriend."

"Exactly." I leaned over Butch and kissed Adam again. "Should we let her out now?"

"Haley? You have her stuffed in a closet somewhere?"

"I'm going to let *Pookie* out now."

"Great idea." He winked.

I quietly slipped down the hall and opened my bedroom door. Pookie had been waiting. She stalked out like she was on a hunt. When she reached the living room, she slowed.

Butch was the first to notice because Sundance was too intent on winning the game of tug of war.

Pookie approached Butch. She seemed more curious than mad. He leaned out to sniff her. And that scared her. She hissed. Her tail frizzed, and she took a swipe at his nose.

Butch sat up and backed away. Poor dog. He looked emotionally wounded.

"Pookie, be nice. Butch won't hurt you." I thought I sounded pretty convincing.

Sundance spotted Pookie and did a little jig.

Adam wrapped his arms around me from behind.

"Has he ever seen a cat before?" It took all my willpower not to scoop Pookie up and rush her back to my bedroom.

"Not since I've had him. Sundance thinks every living thing is another potential friend."

Sundance jumped closer to Pookie, putting his nose to the floor. She hissed, and he jumped again, his tail whooshing back and forth. To Sundance, this was a game.

If I had to guess based on the extended claws, Pookie didn't agree.

Getting away from Sundance, she ran closer to Butch. And he didn't like that at all. In the blink of an eye, he jumped on the end table and knocked over my favorite vase, sending it and a dozen roses to the tile floor.

The loud crash sent Pookie tearing out of the room, every bit of her frizzed.

Adam grabbed Sundance before the dog had a chance to go after the cat. "I'm so sorry."

I stared at the glass shards scattered across the floor.

After Adam barked a command, the dogs sheepishly lay down in their beds.

"You okay?" He brushed my arm.

"It was just a vase." If I said it enough times, I'd learn to believe it. I squatted and began collecting the pieces.

"I'll take care of that in a minute. Come here."

Letting him hug me risked a chink in my defenses. But I didn't want him to think I was mad at him. I wasn't. But I was on the brink of getting emotional.

He wrapped his arms around me. In his calming voice, just like the one he'd used that day in the bathroom, he asked, "Where did you get the vase?"

"It belonged to my grandma. It always sat on her end table with these awful plastic flowers stuffed in it." I laughed and sobbed at the same time.

He kissed the top of my head. "Those really stiff plastic flowers?"

"Yeah. Those. Even from far away, they didn't look real."

"I can bring you more roses, and I'll do my best to find you another vase just like it." He pulled back and looked me in the face. "But I know it won't be the same. I'm sorry."

"And they hate each other." I'd had such high hopes in spite of my worry.

Sundance yipped, and without turning around, Adam said, "Stay in your bed." He kissed my forehead. "They'll need time. Let me get this cleaned up." He sighed.

"I'll help you." I grabbed the broom and dustpan.

Adam gathered the roses. "I don't get why Butch acted like such a big baby."

"Because he got scratched on the nose."

He gathered the glass into the dustpan. "But he should realize that he's bigger than she is . . . by a lot!"

"Why do you sound irritated?" I admit it. I probably shouldn't have laughed at that moment.

He scowled as he dropped the glass in the trash. "I'm not irritated, but it's just silly."

Butch whined, and we both turned around.

Pookie was curled up on his doggie bed, and poor Butch was still on his bed but not at all happy about the company.

Adam groaned. "Really, Butch? She's little. I know the claws hurt, but that's no reason to cry."

"They aren't fighting."

"But I think she knows she's torturing my dog." Adam poked me in the side.

"She's evil that way." I sat on the sofa and patted the cushion beside me. "Come here, Butch."

He ran across the room and jumped up next to me, glad that I'd saved him from the big, bad cat."

"Be nice, Sundance. If you come on too strong, she'll scratch you too."

Sundance inched off his bed and closer to Pookie. She didn't run away. Maybe this day wouldn't end horribly.

"What do you say we watch a movie and let them hang out?" Adam plopped down next to me.

"I like that idea."

Besides Butch being a bit skittish, they were getting along. What could go wrong now? I winced as the thought gelled. Why did I even think of questions like that?

CHAPTER 18

Holding up two shirts, I tried to decide which to take on my getaway. When someone knocked at the door, I tossed the clothes on the bed and ran down the hall. Adam must've cut his run short.

I pulled open the door. "Mom."

"Don't act like you're unhappy to see me. I brought you dinner." She carried a casserole dish into the kitchen.

"Just surprised. Usually you call first." Maybe I should've left that last part off.

After sliding the pan into the oven, she turned it on. "It needs to cook for 30 minutes. When the cheese on top is melted, it's ready. And I didn't call because you'd have said you were busy, and I'm tired of not getting the whole story."

"The whole story about what?" I had a pretty good idea what she meant, but asking the question gave me time to think of an excuse, a reason why I hadn't talked much about Adam.

"You wouldn't have met Adam if it weren't for me. I think the least you can do is keep me posted on how things are going."

Indignation clouded my judgment, and I had to count to ten before answering. "It's going fine. I'm not sure what you want me to say."

"Are you still seeing each other?"

"Yes. He'll be here soon. I didn't see the need to call you every time we had a date."

Mom's gaze swept over me. "You aren't letting him see you like that, are you?" Her eye roll was a bit much. "If you want him to stick around—"

I put up my hand. "I'm not having this conversation with you."

Mom woke up every morning before Dad was out of bed. She applied makeup before he saw her. Every. Single. Day.

I'm pretty sure the only time my dad had seen her without makeup was when she was . . . hmm—maybe never. I was not my mom.

She sighed a bit dramatically. "Well, at least now you'll have something to feed him. But you should only have one piece. That baggy shirt already makes you look heavy. Guys don't like that."

All rational thought left, and my tongue started wagging. "Mom, you are not the reason, I met Adam. Mr. Raymond is. When that tree fell, I was taking a bubble bath and ended up trapped in the bathtub. Adam rescued me." It was useless to stop talking now. "He's seen me at my absolute worst. And he's still here." I propped my fists on my hips. "Any questions?"

Keys jingled and the front door opened. "It's me. I brought dessert." Adam walked into the kitchen and froze when he saw my posture. "Hi, Mrs. Taylor. How are you?"

Mom's eyes widened. "He has a key?"

Adam paled. "I'm watching Pookie this weekend."

"You don't need to explain. Yes, he has a key. He rescued me from the bathtub, and he brings me sweets." I marched over to Adam and clasped his hand. "What else do you want to know?"

He squeezed my hand and set a chocolate swirl cheesecake on the counter. "I'll be in the living room. Y'all can talk."

Pookie scampered up and started climbing Adam's jeans.

"Don't do that, kitty. Even through denim, your claws hurt." He carried her out of the room.

Mom watched him leave then turned to me. "He got rid of his dogs?"

"No." The less said on that subject the better.

"You said you'd never date a guy with a dog. Since high school, you've been saying that."

"I changed my mind."

Had she seen Adam? I'd have been stupid not to change my mind.

She pulled her keys out of her pocket. "I'm sorry I bothered you."

"You didn't bother me. I just . . . wanted to set the record straight." I wanted her to stop acting like I owed her and that I needed to try harder to deserve Adam.

And like every other time I stood up for myself, I felt guilty because she acted so hurt.

"Have a good evening. Call if you have time." She spun and walked to the car.

"Thanks for dinner." I waved, determined not to let her get to me.

When I walked into the living room, Adam raised an eyebrow. "Cat's outta the bag, I guess."

"I didn't intend to tell her. But when she started in on me about my figure and what guys like, it all just came tumbling out."

A lopsided grin spread across his face. "I know what *this guy* likes, and your figure is *definitely* on that list."

Heat flooded my cheeks, and he chuckled.

"How long until dinner is finished? I thought I saw the oven on." He rested his hands on my hips and tugged me closer.

"Probably another twenty minutes or so. Mom brought it."

"Let's have dessert first." His smoldering gaze made me wonder what he meant by dessert.

"Do you mean the cheesecake?"

He nodded. "What did you think I meant?"

I shrugged. "That looked like chocolate swirl, not plain."

"I figure, since you gave me a chance in spite of my dogs, I should give chocolate swirl cheesecake a chance." His hands glided over my hips and up to my waist. "I read in the manual that relationships are about give and take."

"Have you ever tasted chocolate swirl cheesecake?"

"Nope. I liked plain. I didn't see the need to branch out." His breath tickled my neck as he dropped a few kisses below my ear. "But now I do."

"I think you are seriously the most romantic man alive."

Laughing, he continued dropping kisses. "Just don't tell the guys at the station. I'd never hear the end of it."

"Do they know?"

He trailed his fingertips down my arms and laced his fingers with mine. "That I have a girlfriend? Yes. They figured that out when I started slipping outside to talk on the phone."

"What about the other part?"

"Harper knows." He pressed a kiss into the palm of my hand. "But I didn't see the point in mentioning it to the other guys."

"I love you for that."

Adam arched his back and whispered an obscenity. "Pookie, I've asked you not to do that."

I unhooked her claws from his jeans and picked her up.

"It's my turn for cuddles. You already had your treats." I set Pookie on the couch.

Adam rubbed his leg. "We should grab that dessert before dinner is ready. Then maybe you can show me what other kind of dessert you were thinking about."

I swatted his arm. "I'm sure you'd love to know."

∽

Why did work always keep me late when I had someplace to be? I threw my purse in the car and dropped into the driver's seat. I needed to grab my luggage and toss more food in Pookie's bowl. I didn't doubt Adam would take care of her, but I'd never left her for the weekend before.

I called him before backing out. "Hi. I'm just leaving the office. I'm rushing home, then Haley will be picking me up. I left her number on the fridge just in case you can't reach me on my phone."

"You sound nervous. Like you don't trust me to take care of your cat." His tone dripped with humor.

"I trust you. And I promise to call."

"Eve, just go have fun. You know I'll happily take your call anytime, but I don't want to intrude on your weekend. I will miss you though."

"When you check on Pookie later, please ask her nicely not to tear my house apart."

"If you'd like, I can keep her at my place for the weekend."

"I'm sure she'd be fine at the house, but if you don't mind and if Javi doesn't mind, I'd like that. I can pack up her stuff as soon as I get home."

"I don't mind, and Javi is gone for the weekend. But you sound like you're in a hurry. Why don't you give me a list? I'll gather the stuff."

"You don't mind? I feel like I'm asking so much of you."

"Not at all."

"I can text you a list when I get home." I tried to think of everything Pookie would need.

That same calming voice he used the first day we met floated through the line. "I have time and a pen. Just tell me." I listed off what she'd need and where it was. "I'll be home in two minutes, and if I think of anything else, I'll call you."

"All right. Love you. Have a great time." The call ended.

I wasn't going to be that clingy girlfriend who moped about spending time apart. But I would miss him.

We talked every day on the phone, and when he wasn't working, he came over for dinner. He'd bring the dogs with him sometimes. I still wasn't crazy about them, but they were growing on me . . . a little.

I turned onto my street and smiled as the house came into view. Adam's truck sat in the driveway. But the cab was empty.

He stood in the doorway, grinning. "I hope you don't mind that I let myself in."

"Not a bit."

"I stopped in to say goodbye and to pick up Pookie."

I wrapped my arms around his neck. "You're going to miss me, aren't you?"

"I already said I would." He pressed a quick kiss to my lips then picked up a huge gift bag off the entry table. "Here. This is for you. For the weekend."

More than curious, I yanked the tissue out of the top and grinned at the weekend survival kit—everything I'd need to pamper myself during the getawawy. "How did you know I liked all this stuff? I mean, some of these I haven't had since we started dating. And this is the brand of nail polish I use. How did you know?"

"Haley."

"I just wrote the number on the fridge this morning."

Twinkles danced in his brown eyes. "I know where she lives. I made sure to toss in a few things she likes too. I hope that color is okay."

I usually opted for softer colors, ones that didn't stand out. I had on occasion worn a vivid red. But never had I chosen a bright tangerine. After this weekend, my fingernails and toenails would be that color. "It's gorgeous."

"I know it's not what you usually wear. I just thought it would look good on you." He pushed the bag closer. "And I trust y'all will drink responsibly. I picked out a couple bottles of wine. A white and a blush. Blush just seemed like something ladies would drink on a girls' weekend."

"Smart man. I so want to drag you to the sofa and kiss you until my lips burn, but then Haley would be irritated with me for making us late. Raincheck?"

He rubbed at his stubble and flashed that lopsided grin. "Most definitely."

CHAPTER 19

Haley curled up at the end of the sofa, cradling her glass of wine. "This stuff is great. I need to remember to take a picture of the label."

"I still can't believe you didn't say anything to me about Adam showing up at your apartment." I stacked dry salami and cheddar cheese on a cracker. "But he did a great job shopping for treats."

"I'm glad he pulled off the surprise." Haley twisted the glass in her hand, watching the ripples dance across the top. "You're all in with him, right? I mean, it's obvious he's nuts about you. And typically, that leads to a question being popped. Are you ready to live with dogs?"

I wanted to be. "His dogs are nice. They usually listen when I ask them to stop licking or stay down."

"That wasn't an answer to my question." She sipped her wine. "You realize that now that you've asked him to watch Pookie, it's fair game for him to ask you to keep the dogs, right?"

I hadn't exactly thought of it like that. "The dogs stay with Javi when Adam is working."

"I get why you like Adam. Gosh, all anyone has to do is look at him, and they'd understand that. But I know you. You don't like dogs. How is this going to work? Really."

To say I felt blindsided was a complete understatement. "Have you been talking to my mom?"

"No, I haven't. And I'm not your mom. I'm your best friend. I want you to be happy. But I also don't want you to break this poor guy's heart."

"Is this why you wanted to have a girls' weekend?"

"Yes. And then he pulled that stunt getting you all the treats, which made it more imperative that I talk to you about it."

"People can change their minds."

"About whether they like asparagus maybe, but cat people don't become dog people. It doesn't happen."

I downed the last of my wine and pictured Adam sprawled on the floor, playing with the dogs. No matter what scenario my imagination dreamed up, I couldn't picture myself doing that. "I'm going to head to bed."

"It's not even ten. Don't do that."

I poured myself another half a glass. "Using small words, tell me what you think I should do."

"You should stay up until at least midnight." She flashed a teasing grin, but it fell away quickly when I didn't react. "You should break it off before that man gets down on one knee. That's what I think."

"Are you offering advice because you want the best for me or because you're jealous of my good thing?" I should never have asked that question, but pain could be funny that way. It prompted unbridled honesty.

Hurt flashed in Haley's eyes. "I'm going to pretend you didn't just say that. We should move on to a different topic. But before we do, I'll throw this out there. Volunteer to keep his dogs. See how it goes. You'll know then if things will work." She leaned forward. "Eve, I want it to work out for the two of you. I really do. But I also want you to be happy, and not happy with a side of bothered."

"I told Mom how Adam and I met."

Haley flopped back on the sofa. "And?"

"I told her yesterday. We haven't talked since." I'd pushed the worry about that to the side, and though like a good dog, the worry stayed shoved to the side, it gnawed on that part of my brain endlessly.

Haley giggled. "I really wanted to be there when she heard the story."

I wasn't quite ready to laugh about it. "I didn't give her the play by play. Just the basic highlights."

"Why would you tell your mom? Does Adam know? If not, you should tell him because what if he bumps into your dad somewhere? That could be interesting."

"Adam knows. I lost my temper when she started in on me. She brought up the dog thing too."

"We aren't talking about that anymore tonight." Haley jumped up and pulled the leftover chocolate swirl cheesecake out of the fridge. "Let's have dessert then do our nails."

"Sounds good."

∼

I TEXTED ADAM AS HALEY PULLED OUT OF THE DRIVEWAY. *Leaving now. Should be home in about an hour.*

You going to stop for dinner?

No. We're ready to be home.

See you soon.

Haley shot me a look. "Adam?"

"Just letting him know we're on our way. He's probably ready to send Pookie home."

"Are you going to offer to dog-sit?"

"Yes." I wasn't sure when, but I'd offer. And hopefully, I'd still be in love when Adam came to pick them up.

"I'd offer to come help, but you need to do it on your own." Haley turned up the radio. "This is a good song."

With music blaring, we drove home. I had lots to think about.

When we pulled up to my place, Haley sighed. "Oh look, Adam's here."

"You should come in for a bit." I wasn't sure I wanted her to, but it was polite to offer.

"Just for a bit."

I pushed open the door and was greeted by a delicious aroma. "I'm home. It smells amazing."

Butch barreled toward me then stopped before jumping on me.

"Hey, boy. This is Haley."

She dropped to her knees and loved on Butch. "You are a handsome doggie, aren't you?"

I left her with the dog. "Hey there. Thanks for cooking."

Adam winked. "It was a good excuse to spend a little time with you. But I made enough for Haley too. Did y'all have fun?"

"Yeah."

He furrowed his brow. "That didn't sound very convincing."

"I'm starved. How long until it's ready?"

"It needs another two minutes. And your avoidance skills leave a lot to be desired. Should I be worried?"

"We'll talk more later. I should check on Haley." I found her rolling on the living room floor with Butch licking her face and Sundance waiting for her to pick up the rope toy.

She looked perfectly comfortable.

"Want to stay for dinner?" I crossed my arms, wishing I didn't feel like crying.

She grinned. "Sure. You're right. These are great dogs. I'm jealous."

"It'll be ready in a minute." I walked back into the kitchen. "Where's Pookie?"

"She took off as soon as we got home. I'm not sure where she is." Adam transferred food to a platter. "But she made it back here alive."

"I'm going to find her really quick." I poked my head into some of her favorite hiding spots, but she wasn't there. I finally found her curled up on my pillow. "Hello, sweet girl. Did you miss me?"

She flipped the end of her tail and rolled onto her back, demanding belly scratches.

"I missed you too."

CHAPTER 20

I snuggled up next to Adam. "I don't want to keep you. I know you have to be at the station early."

"Talk to me." He threaded his fingers through my hair. "What happened this weekend?"

As if sensing my thoughts, Butch climbed up next to me.

"I don't want to get into the details of it, but I'll pet sit Butch and Sundance the next time you need me to."

Adam blinked and cocked his head. "I'm missing something. What does keeping the dogs have to do with your weekend?"

"I just think it's important that I do that."

"You mean Haley thinks it's important." He lifted my chin. "That's what this is about?"

"Everyone likes to remind me about my issues with dogs. But no one wants to believe that people can change."

"You don't have to prove yourself to me, Eve."

"But I kind of need to prove myself to me." I met his gaze, hoping the emotions bubbling in my heart were readable in my eyes. "So, if you trust me to take care of them, I'd like to."

"I work this coming Saturday and Sunday. Want to keep them this weekend?"

"Yes. You'll have to let me know what I need to get."

"About that raincheck..."

I trailed a finger through his whiskers. "You didn't shave all weekend, did you?"

"All the better to burn your lips, my dear."

∼

On Friday, I stood in the living room, scanning every visible surface. Was there anything else breakable that needed to be put up, far away from the dogs?

"Pookie, are you ready for this?"

Kitty tore around the room like something was chasing her. Or maybe she was just excited about having her friends come over. Adam had mentioned more than once about how well things had gone over the weekend with them all together.

I was both nervous and excited about dog-sitting. And since Adam didn't have to go to work until tomorrow morning, tonight would be easy. He'd be around to help with the transition. Well, not all night.

A quick peek into the oven verified that I hadn't made a disaster of dinner. And so far, I'd managed to keep Pookie out of the doggie treats I bought at a local pet boutique. They looked tempting even to me.

Adam's truck pulled into the driveway, and I ran for the door. Watching him carry those doggie beds was a treat all its own.

He grinned as he walked toward the house, those arm muscles well defined. "You ready for this?"

"As ready as I'll ever be. Put those wherever."

He stopped before going inside and leaned in for a kiss. "I brought you something."

"You didn't have to do that."

"Maybe I just like getting you things." He winked before walking inside.

Butch and Sundance jumped around the inside of the truck, ready to be let out.

"Should I let them out of the truck?"

Adam laughed. "Sure. They are very excited about coming back over here."

"Sundance is probably excited about seeing Pookie." I glanced back as I walked to the truck.

He leaned against the porch railing. "And Butch is not."

I yanked open the door, and the dogs climbed over each other to get out. Sundance licked my hand then bolted for the door. He could probably smell the cat. Butch sat, staring at me. His mouth moved like he was trying his best to not lick me.

Both of the dogs were sweet, but Butch seemed determined to win me over.

I leaned down and rested my forehead against his. "You're going to make this easy on me, right?"

His tail slapped the walkway. I think that was his version of a yes.

Adam grabbed a gift bag out of the front seat then locked the truck. "Thanks for making dinner."

"You made it last night. Didn't the manual say relationships were supposed to be a give and take?" I held his hand as we walked inside.

"True." He set the gift bag on the table. "Open it."

Before I had a chance, Sundance and Pookie tore through the kitchen.

"Whoa! I hope that was a friendly chase." I peeked into the living room.

Adam called Pookie as he slipped the treat bag out of his back pocket. "Where's my sweet girl?"

It irritated me that she came running. When I called her, she didn't budge.

Pookie made it a few inches up his pant leg before Adam scooped her up. "Don't climb my leg, darlin'." He fed her a few treats.

If he kept that up, she'd never stop climbing his leg.

I turned my focus back to the bag. "Survival kits two weekends in a row! We loved this wine."

"I figured you might need a glass." He took the bottle and tucked it in the fridge. "That way it will be chilled when you need it."

"Thanks. And chocolate. Yum!" I continued pulling treats and snacks out of the bag. "Bubble bath, really?"

"You still avoiding them?"

I was, which was stupid. But soaking in a warm bubble bath seemed like inviting lightning to strike twice. "Maybe."

"Anything I can do to help with that?" His brown eyes twinkled.

Shaking my head, I pulled dinner out of the oven. "No. There isn't."

He let loose a chuckle as he set the table. "I didn't think so, but I knew asking would turn your cheeks that beautiful shade of red."

"Have a seat and let's eat." I didn't mind the teasing. But when he talked like that, it did make me want more than having dinner in the evening and spending weekends together when he wasn't working.

I needed this doggie sleepover to go well if Adam and I were going to move down that road. He hadn't said that, but we both knew it was true.

∼

Adam loved on the dogs before walking to the door. He'd lingered later than normal, which I liked, but he was probably nervous about leaving them with me.

He pulled me close. "I'll leave my ringer on. If you need *anything*, call me. Okay?"

I inched up on my toes and kissed him like the dogs weren't looking. "What if I need that?"

"I'll violate traffic laws on my way over." He gave me another kiss. "Love you."

"Love you too."

Once he was in the truck, I locked the door. "Okay boys, I'm going to get ready for bed, but first, I'll let you go outside to do your business. Then it's bedtime."

They cocked their heads like they were listening intently, but I doubted they understood a single word.

I let them out, and while they did their business and barked at the moon, I filled Pookie's bowl. I'd moved her bowl into the other room so that the dogs didn't eat her food.

"Shh. People are trying to sleep. Come back inside." I stepped back as they barreled toward the door.

When they made it inside, I pointed at their beds. "Go to bed."

Butch obeyed immediately. Sundance wandered down the hall, probably looking for Pookie.

"Sundance, bed."

He trudged to his big, green doggie bed and climbed in.

"Night. Be good."

I left my bedroom door open a crack. That way, I could hear if something went horribly wrong.

But dogs weren't like cats. They slept at night, right?

CHAPTER 21

I looked at my phone, sure that it had to be almost morning. But it wasn't. Only ten minutes had passed since I'd last checked the time.

The dogs had been very quiet. Were they too quiet?

I pulled on a pair of leggings. As if the dogs would care if I was only in a t-shirt—Adam's t-shirt. I tiptoed down the hall. If they were sleeping, I didn't want to wake them.

Pookie and Sundance were snuggled together. Butch's tail started wagging when he spotted me.

"Stay in your bed. I was just checking on you." I hurried back down the hall. Sleep wasn't optional. I flopped onto my back and squeezed my eyes closed. In my mind, I conjured up a green pasture and a white picket fence. Sleep-inducing, jumping sheep would send me to dreamland.

The first little sheep launched himself over the little fence, and something big shook my bed.

My imagination wasn't that good. I had a guess about what sort of creature had joined me in bed.

Butch stood over me, his nose right in my face.

Apparently "stay in your bed" sounded like an invitation to him.

Hesitantly, he licked my face.

Slow breaths helped me control my panic. With him standing on the blankets, I was trapped.

"I don't like this. Please move." Talking to him like he was a person did nothing to change the situation. I wriggled an arm free and shoved on him. "Get off of me."

The more I talked, the faster his tail wagged.

"Down, Butch."

With his tail whooshing back and forth, he lay down on top of me.

"Do you weigh two hundred pounds? Yikes, you're heavy." In an impulsive act of desperation, I patted the bed next to me. "Come over here."

Thankfully, he obeyed. Situating himself next to my hand, he licked it over and over.

"I like you too. Please go to sleep." I rolled onto my side.

He inched closer until his head was against my shoulder.

This doggie sleepover was going better than I'd expected. With Butch next to me, I finally slept.

Growling woke me up. The room was still dark. But there was just enough light to see that Butch was staring at the window. A low growl rumbled in his chest.

The logical side of my brain said that a raccoon or opossum was out for a nightly stroll, but the other part of my brain imagined a knife-wielding prowler, one who was looking for an unsecured entry point.

"What is it, boy?"

Butch jumped off the bed and positioned himself in front of the window. The blinds were moving, but he hadn't touched them.

I slid the covers back, trying to formulate a plan.

What was I going to do if someone was in my house?

That's when I thought about the big dog in front of me. He was acting as my defender. I should let him.

"Go get it, Butch."

He launched toward the window. The blinds rattled, and a very frizzed Pookie jumped out.

I screamed.

Butch and Pookie took off in opposite directions. And Sundance, who was late to the party, ran up the hall, barking.

That was when I gave up on the idea of sleep. Coffee would have to suffice.

While coffee brewed, I dug through the survival kit and grabbed a few chocolates. Adam had purchased the jumbo-size box. That added yet another item to the list of reasons I loved that man.

With a steaming mug of coffee in hand, I settled on the sofa with a book.

Reading did the trick. Even loaded with caffeine, I fell asleep.

Sometime later, Butch's tail knocked against the sofa, or was that someone knocking? I patted him without opening my eyes, and the knocking stopped.

Keys jingled. It was either Adam or my parents. And I hoped beyond hope that it wasn't my parents.

"You okay? Can I come in?" Adam wasn't using his calm soothing voice.

"I'm in the living room." I opened one eye. "Aren't you supposed to be at work?"

"You said to call you first thing. I did, but you didn't answer. So I took a detour on my way to work." He greeted his ecstatic dogs.

I wasn't the only one who missed him when he wasn't around. "Sorry. I left my phone in my room when I wandered out here. Things went okay."

He sat down beside me, and humor appeared as little creases near his eyes. "You're wearing my shirt."

"You gave it to me. I sleep in it almost every night." I stretched. "Want me to make you coffee?"

"I need to run. Traffic was already getting bad." He stepped closer.

I slipped my arms around his waist. "I managed to keep them alive all night."

"Glad it went well." He gave me a quick kiss. "I'll be back here Monday as soon as I get off. Will you still be here?"

"I leave for work about eight."

"Okay. Love you." He raced back out to his truck.

I laughed when I saw Sundance and Butch staring out the front window. "I know. I miss him too. But he'll be back in a couple of days. Until then, you're stuck with me."

Butch followed me to the couch and curled up next to me.

"Tonight, you have to sleep in your own bed, okay?"

He dropped his head onto the cushion and looked at me.

I didn't hold out high hopes.

~

Sunday night, I crawled into bed, eager to tell Adam how well it had gone. We'd talked on the phone, but I wanted to see his reaction when I confessed that I sort of liked having the dogs around.

Saturday night had gone so well, I expected Sunday night would be just as smooth.

Of course that assumption was misguided.

A dog crying woke me up about two-thirty. I trudged out to the living room and shook my head. Pookie lay curled up in the middle of Butch's bed. That poor dog looked so forlorn. His whine grew louder when he saw me.

"Pookie, get out of his bed. You know he doesn't want you there."

Without lifting her head, she flicked her tail.

"Go sleep with Sundance. He likes you. Butch is scared of you because you do things like this to him."

Her eyes drooped closed, and it was clear she had no intention of listening to me.

I picked her up. "Come into my room and leave that doggie alone."

Butch happily curled up in his bed, and Pookie and I went back to my room. I was back to sleep in a matter of minutes, but then the whining started again.

Since Pookie was no longer in my bed, I could guess why Butch was upset. I stopped in the kitchen and pulled the box of chocolates out of the bag. Being awakened in the middle of the night earned me a special treat.

"Pookie, are you bothering him again?"

Yes, she was. Back in the center of his bed, she was now sprawled on her back. What a tease.

"Butch, just come sleep in my bed. I'll close that menace out for the rest of the night."

Sundance lay there, still snoring. It amazed me what that dog could sleep through.

Butch followed me back to bed and curled up beside me. Without a kitty to bother us, we drifted off to sleep.

CHAPTER 22

Somehow, I slept through my alarm. I needed to be up and ready when Adam arrived. But the first thing I needed was coffee.

I called Haley as I bounced down the hall. I was a much more chipper version of my usual morning self, and a little bit of gloating was in order. I'd accepted the challenge, and I'd survived. More than survived, I let a dog sleep in my bed. Twice. "Good morning, I'm calling to report that I kept the dogs all weekend and—Oh no!"

Sundance lay on the kitchen floor with dog puke all around him. Next to him was my box of chocolates. Empty. Pookie lay on top of him, and if a cat could look worried, she did.

"What's wrong?" Haley echoed the panic I felt.

"Sundance ate my chocolates. And he's puked all over the kitchen floor." I gathered my hair into a ponytail as if that would help me think.

"Chocolate is poisonous to dogs. You have to get him to a vet. Now!"

"That would've been good information to have before.

Okay, I need to call Adam. I'll talk to you later." I dialed Adam, hoping he wasn't out on an emergency.

He answered right away. "Hi. I'm walking to my truck right now. How'd it go?"

"Sundance ate some of the chocolates. He's sick. I'm going to rush him to the vet."

"There's an emergency vet about a mile from your place. The one near the gas station. Know the place?"

"In the same strip mall with the taco shop?"

"Yeah. That's the one."

I stroked Sundance on the head. "I'll meet you there." I stuffed the phone in the pocket of my leggings. Pockets on leggings were one of the greatest inventions since smartphones. And why was I thinking about that now? Rambling thoughts wouldn't help me. I needed to stay focused.

I moved Pookie off to the side. "Stay out of the yuck, please."

She retreated under the table and curled up beside Butch. Amazingly, he didn't even flinch.

"Come on, Sundance baby. Let's go for a ride." I motioned for him to stand up.

His tail wagged a little, and he stood. I grabbed his collar and led him out of the kitchen. Once I had my keys and purse, I loaded Sundance into my car.

I rolled my window partway down. The car now reeked of vomit, and I was trying desperately not to add to it.

At the vet's office, Sundance didn't want to get out of the car. He looked worse than before. The normally excitable Husky lay on the backseat, moving only his eyes.

I wrapped my arms around him and dragged him to the edge of the seat. "Work with me, Sundance. You aren't exactly light. And I'm not exactly strong."

Picking him up wouldn't be easy. I reminded myself to lift

with my knees as I stood up. After kicking the car door closed, I hobbled toward the clinic door.

Thankfully, an alert tech spotted me and let me in. "Hi. What's wrong with him?"

"It's my boyfriend's dog. He got into my chocolate. When I found him, he'd thrown up all over the floor." I felt the need to say that even though it was probably obvious because the vomit was all over me.

"Bring him in here." She stepped into a small exam room and pointed at a vinyl-covered bench. "I'll get the vet."

I laid Sundance down but kept an arm wrapped around him. "You have to be okay, buddy. I'm sorry I left those chocolates where you could reach them. I didn't know."

Tears stung my eyes. If Sundance didn't make it, Adam would never forgive me. If I couldn't keep a dog alive for one weekend, how would he want to marry me? Forget the idea of children.

Whoa! That thought train sure jumped the tracks.

I blinked back tears. "Please don't die." I kissed the top of his head, one of the few spots not covered in puke.

Adam's voice carried in from the lobby, so I stepped away from Sundance and poked my head out. "We're in here."

He came running in, calling out a promise to fill out the paperwork in a minute. He glanced at me then pulled Sundance into his arms. "Hey there. The vet is going to make you feel better, okay?"

"The tech said he'd be in soon." I choked out the last word. "I'm sorry."

Adam nodded but didn't meet my gaze.

"I'll be in the waiting area." I left Adam with his dog and took a seat in one of the hard plastic chairs. Tears streamed down my cheeks. Sobbing and covered in dog puke, I must've been quite the sight.

"Ma'am, if you'd like to wash your hands, the bathroom is right there." The receptionist pointed at a door.

I knew a hint when I heard one. "Thanks." I slipped inside and washed my face and hands.

When I walked back out, Adam was in a chair, filling out paperwork.

"Where's Sundance? Is he okay?" I dropped into the chair next to him and rested my hand on his arm.

He pinched his lips together and continued writing.

I understood, but it hurt worse than getting a sticker poked in the bottom of my foot. "Do you want me to leave?"

Focused on the clipboard, he shook his head. "They took Sundance into the back. He'll get his stomach pumped. It's too soon to know if he'll be okay."

"I'm so sorry. I want to hug you, but I'm nasty."

He continued scrawling on that stupid paper. "Why don't you head home? I'll be over in a bit to pick up Butch."

"I want to stay, but I'm not even sure I locked my house." I ignored the part about picking up Butch, hoping that didn't signal an end to our relationship.

I couldn't blame Adam if it did, but I'd cry myself to sleep for a month at least. And I couldn't even think about telling my mom.

"Just go. Check the house. Take a shower. I'll be over in a bit."

I kissed his cheek. "Are you okay to drive?"

"I'm fine." That was a flat out lie, but arguing wouldn't change the answer.

I walked back out to the car, glad that my purse was still where I'd left it. I dialed my boss before backing out.

"Mindy, I'm not going to make it in today. I was pet sitting, and one of the dogs got into chocolate—"

"Oh no. Chocolate is poison to dogs. Is he okay?"

How did everyone in the world except me know about chocolate being poison?

I turned onto my street, hoping I'd at least closed my front door. Losing the other dog wouldn't be a good way to win back Adam's affections. "We don't know yet. The vet is going to keep him for a while. He'll call us later."

"No worries about not coming in. I hope the doggie is okay." Mindy sounded distracted.

"Me too. It's my boyfriend's dog."

"Yikes. That's not good. Listen, I need to run. I'll talk to you later." She ended the call.

When I parked in the driveway, I called Haley. "Sundance is at the vet. Adam hardly spoke to me. What am I going to do if I killed his dog?"

"You'll need more chocolate."

"That's not funny!" I pushed the door open and walked around looking for Butch and Pookie.

"I wasn't trying to be funny. People cope differently. Some women drink straight tequila; others indulge in chocolate. You are definitely one of the eating-chocolate variety.

I found Butch and Pookie curled up together in Sundance's bed. "Maybe. I need a shower then I have a mess to clean up."

"Are you okay?"

"No. I'm not okay. I need to let you go. Adam is calling me." I switched to the other call. "Hi. Any news?"

"The vet wants to know how long ago he ingested it. Do you have any idea?"

"Sometime after two-thirty. I was up at that time, and he was asleep in his bed. The chocolates were still in the box. After that Butch crawled in bed with me, and I closed the door to keep Pookie out. That's why I didn't hear Sundance getting into stuff."

"You may have gotten him here in time." He ended the call without another word.

Not only did I feel horrible because Sundance was sick, but Adam was so distant. He was worried, but was he mad?

I wandered back to take a shower. I could just as easily worry while getting clean as I could covered in yuck.

So much soap was required. Finally, after multiple scrubbings and two rounds of shampoo in my hair, I no longer reeked. Sobbing didn't help me shower quickly either.

After drying off, I threw on shorts and a grubby t-shirt. The next chore wouldn't be fun.

Adam was on his hands and knees in the kitchen. "Hey, I'm almost finished cleaning this up. I'm sorry he messed up your floor."

"I'll do that. You have no reason to be sorry."

He gave a small grunt without looking up.

I touched his back. "Please look at me."

Sad brown eyes focused on me as he stood. "I'm really worried."

"Me too. I feel horrible." I leaned in to hug him.

He shook his head and looked down at his shirt. "You don't want to do that."

I did, actually. "Do you have clothes with you? Go shower. I'll clean up the rest."

He nodded. "I haven't even checked on Butch to see if he needs a bath."

"I'll check on them. Bathing Pookie will be so fun."

Adam gave a slight chuckle. "Yeah."

He closed himself in the bathroom, and I peeked into the living room. Butch and Pookie were still lying in the doggie bed and looking at me like I'd just ruined Christmas.

While Adam showered, I mopped the kitchen. When the water stopped, it occurred to me that he hadn't taken anything into the bathroom with him. Did he plan to put on dirty clothes? Why bother to shower if he was going to put those puke-covered clothes back on?

The bathroom door opened, and with a fluffy, coral-colored towel wrapped around him, he leaned out. "I forgot to grab my bag out of the truck. Would you mind?" He held out his keys.

I stood there, staring at his chest. "Sorry. Did you say something?"

"Very funny." He jingled the keys. "Will you grab my bag?"

Grinning, I took the keys.

"And now we're even, right?" He motioned to his still-damp body. "Only difference is I'm not in the tub."

"You have a giant towel. That's a pretty big difference." I ran out to the truck, thankful for the little bit of laughter. When I walked back inside, I set the bag a few paces from the bathroom door. "The bag is outside the door." Leaning against the wall, I waited.

For once, I wasn't the one blushing.

He gripped his towel, holding it in place. "I'm glad this amuses you."

"You could raise money for charity if you posed like that for a firemen calendar. Oh! You could be holding Pookie."

"I'm all for charity, but I think I'll pass." He stepped back into the bathroom then peeked back out. "But I am flattered."

I left him to get dressed.

After he'd put on clean clothes, he walked out to the living room. "Mind if I wash these?"

"Just drop them in the washer. My clothes are already in there." I followed him into the laundry room and started the load. "I checked Pookie and Butch. Somehow, they managed to stay out of it. At least they don't smell like they got into the mess."

"That's good news." He nodded toward the living room. "Sorry I made you late for work."

I followed him into the other room. "I told them I wouldn't be in today." I finally gave Adam the hug I'd been craving. "I feel horrible. I didn't know about the chocolate being poison. If I'd known, I would've put it up someplace way out of his reach. I don't want you to hate me."

He kissed the top of my head. "Did you really let Butch sleep with you?"

"He wouldn't quit whining. Pookie kept sleeping in his bed, so I figured that was the only way to get sleep. But it looks like the two of them have figured it out. They both hate me."

"I don't think they hate you, Eve."

"They do. Watch." I dropped onto the sofa and patted the cushion. "Come here, Butch. Pookie, come curl up over here."

Pookie didn't even lift her head. At least Butch had the courtesy to act like he had to think about it.

Adam grabbed my hand. "First of all, Pookie never comes when you call. Well, except that one time when she was in the tree. And Butch just doesn't know what to think. Sundance is always around."

"I didn't even think of that. Poor doggie." I wiped my eyes, determined not to fall apart.

Butch trotted over and laid his head on my leg. He knew when I needed a doggie hug.

I patted my lap. "Come sit up here."

He climbed up next to me and dropped his head in my lap.

Adam draped an arm around me. "Pookie, come on. There's room for you too."

That darn cat scampered across the room and sat in Adam's lap.

"How did you teach her to do that?"

"It took me all weekend, but she really likes those treats."

"And that's why she's sitting in your lap, silently begging."

Chuckling, he pulled the bag out of his pocket. "These almost went through the wash." After Pookie had eaten her treats, Adam pulled a receipt out of his pocket. "I don't think I've showed you this."

He wadded it up and tossed it across the room, and Pookie ran for it. She batted it around a second then picked it up with her mouth and carried it back to Adam. She dropped it in his lap.

"You taught her to play fetch?" I didn't recognize my own cat.

"Cute, isn't it?"

"You're turning her into a dog."

He chuckled. "What's so bad about that?"

He tossed it over and over, and after bringing it back a few times, Pookie decided she was tired of playing. She stayed in his lap and watched the bit of paper fly across the room, but she didn't chase after it.

It seemed weird having fun without Sundance around.

"How long did the vet say we'd have to wait?" I leaned my head on Adam's shoulder.

He shrugged, and I swear the sun ducked behind a cloud because the room darkened.

"Can you ever forgive me?"

"I don't blame you. I'm the one that brought the chocolate. I should've said something." He rested his head on mine. "Thanks for staying with me."

I kissed his cheek.

"You *really* let Butch sleep with you?"

"Why do you keep asking me that? Yes. Even after he pinned me to the bed and licked my face."

"Oh no. What did you do?" He ran his fingers through my hair.

"I was authoritative like you suggested. I told him to get down."

"And?"

I patted Butch. "He laid himself down on top of me."

Adam shook his head. "But you figured it out."

"I did." I'd enjoyed having them around way more than I expected.

"Did you like having them here?" He tucked a strand of hair behind my ear.

"I do." I was anything but subtle. I might as well have dropped to my knees and begged him to marry me, but honesty was supposed to be the best policy.

Adam's phone rang, and he lunged for it. "Hello."

I held my breath and waited for good news. It had to be good news.

"Thank you. Yes, I will." Adam ended the call. "Sundance is doing okay. They think he'll make it, but they want to keep him overnight."

"So it's good news, right?"

"So far, yes. You got him to the vet in time." His shoulders relaxed. "Thank you."

The morning ended much better than it had started.

CHAPTER 23

I sat on the counter, watching Adam cook. "If you want to stay close to the vet clinic, I don't mind if you stay here tonight." Even after spending all day together, I wasn't ready for him to leave. "In the guest room."

He glanced up from the cutting board. "If you don't mind, I think I'd like to be *close to the vet clinic*." He emphasized his last few words. "Thanks for asking."

"When the vet tech called late this afternoon, I got super worried."

"I know. But it sounds like he's almost back to normal." Adam tossed the diced tomato into the pan. "Keeping him overnight is just a precaution."

"I'm glad he's okay. And that we're okay."

"I'm sorry if at any point you thought we weren't. I meant every word written on that mug, Eve."

"I love you too."

"Staying here will be good because then I can drive you to get your car."

"Getting it detailed was a great idea. Those poor guys. It smelled awful." I admired the tangerine color on my toes. It did look good on me. "I was thinking we might need to do a family dinner again."

He crinkled his nose. "You think we need to? So soon?"

"We had them over months ago. What if we invited our families over here for Thanksgiving?" I'd been thinking about it before the disaster with the chocolate. It would be an easy way to let the family know Adam and I were serious. I might even love on the dogs while my mother gaped.

"You're a brave woman. But it's not a bad idea. My siblings are at their in-laws this year. They alternate years."

"Same with mine. We could spend Thanksgiving together if we hosted it here. Neither set of parents would be left out. And you could invite Harper."

"He'd like that. I need to check the schedule. I'm not sure if we're on duty that day."

"We can be thankful any day of the week, not just on a Thursday. We'll gather on a day you aren't working."

"I'll help you cook." He wiped his hands and tossed the dish towel over his shoulder. "I can make a stuffing that will bring you to tears."

"That bad, huh?" I leaned close and gave him a quick kiss.

"You going to change back into my shirt before bed?" A smug grin spread across his face.

"I wear it so often, it's going to start falling apart." I slid off the counter and laid out plates and silverware.

He set the food on the trivet in the center of the table. "I'll bring you more shirts. We get them all the time."

"You cook. You bring me goodies. What's not to love about you?"

He wrapped his arms around me. "Absolutely nothing."

After a satisfying meal, we carried dessert to the sofa.

"Let me get this straight, you don't eat your cheesecake plain, but you like plain vanilla ice cream." He kicked his feet up onto the ottoman.

"Yep, I also like it with gummy worms, but I don't have any. But next time I get a cheesecake, I'll try plain. Just for you." I patted the sofa, and Butch climbed up next to me. "I'm not sure how I'm going to sleep tonight."

"You and me both. Have a Scrabble game? We can play until the letters start to blur."

"Sounds like a great plan." I jumped up and ran to the closet. "I haven't played in ages."

Game after game, I beat Adam at Scrabble. Either he was letting me win, or he was distracted by worry.

"I think I'm ready for bed. I can hardly keep my eyes open."

"Yeah. It's late."

He followed me down the hall until we were standing awkwardly outside my room.

"I guess I'll see you in the morning."

"You will." Adam backed me against the wall just outside my bedroom. "Thank you for tonight."

"For beating you at Scrabble?" I ran a finger down the front of his shirt.

"For being you." His head dipped toward mine.

I slid my arms around his neck as our lips met. Dogs and all, Adam was what I wanted.

He broke away and backed up. "I should go that way." He pointed down the hall.

"Wait. Let me get you an extra blanket. I don't want you to be cold."

"How thoughtful." He followed me into the bedroom.

I lifted the lid on my hope chest and pulled out a quilt.

"So that's what's in there."

I pushed him back toward the door. "Just blankets. Nothing scandalous."

He hugged the blanket to his chest. "Thanks."

If he didn't walk away, we'd both still be standing in the hall when the sun came up.

"Goodnight."

"Love you." Adam strode away, leaving a very conflicted-looking Butch alone in the hall.

I laughed. "Hard choice, isn't it?" With my door open a crack, I slid under the covers.

Butch nosed the door open a second later and jumped onto the bed.

Maybe Pookie would sleep in Adam's bed.

∼

THE SMELL OF COFFEE WAFTED DOWN THE HALL. I COULD GET used to waking up to coffee and a hot breakfast. "Morning. Looks like you've been up a while."

"About an hour." He arranged bacon and eggs on two plates.

"What time are you supposed to go get Sundance?"

"They said I could come by any time after seven." He dropped into a chair. "I've downed way too much coffee this morning. Did you know that Pookie catches treats?"

"Haley taught her that."

"Is Haley a dog or a cat person?"

"Yes. But she doesn't have either right now. Her apartment doesn't allow pets."

I glanced at the time. "It's almost seven."

We rushed through breakfast then I pulled on shoes.

Before we walked out, I dropped down in front of Butch. "We're going to pick up Sundance, okay? He'll be home in just a bit."

Butch wagged his tail as if he understood every word.

I kissed him then ran toward the door. "I'm ready."

"They really have grown on you, haven't they?"

"They're as sweet as you are. They just slobber more."

He laughed.

When the vet tech brought Sundance out of the back, I thought my heart might burst. That dog tripped over himself trying to get to Adam.

Adam lifted Sundance off the ground and cradled him like a baby. "You gave us a scare, bud."

Sundance licked Adam's face repeatedly.

Maybe, just maybe, I was becoming a bit of a dog person.

CHAPTER 24

"Tell me again why you decided to host Thanksgiving dinner." Adam laid napkins next to each plate.

"Lots of reasons. It eliminates Mom's favorite threat. If I'm hosting, she'll stop hanging that over my head. And because dinner will be on my turf."

"You're a cat, aren't you?"

"That's important because we chose when to have it. We don't have to wait for Thursday to give thanks."

"I appreciate you planning it around my work schedule."

"You're welcome." I hugged him from behind, burying my face in his back. "I'm sorry Harper couldn't make it, but it's good that he got to go home and see his family." When I pulled back, I scanned the room. "Where did I put my list? I need to make sure I haven't forgotten anything."

"Right here." He waved the piece of paper back and forth. "When are you supposed to put the turkey in the oven?"

The room started to spin. "I didn't. You said you'd cook it in that pot." Had we talked about a different plan? If so, why didn't I remember?

"I'm joking. The oil is almost to temp. Turkey will be cooked in less than an hour."

"Not funny."

"Wrong. That was very funny. But you need to calm down. It'll be fine."

"Right. The stuffing is in the oven. And our moms are bringing the other side dishes. This might work out after all."

Someone knocked, and Adam kissed me. "Smile. It's family time."

∼

WITH BOTH DADS OFFERING HELPFUL ADVICE, ADAM CARVED the turkey.

His mom pulled the sweet potatoes and stuffing out of the oven and slid in the rolls. "These will be ready in about ten minutes."

"I need four straight pins, dear." Mom tucked aluminum foil into a folded napkin.

I dug out my sewing repair kit, hoping there was something helpful in there. "What are you doing?"

"I wanted the table to look pretty, so I'm folding these napkins into turkeys. The pin just holds it all together."

This was the one flaw in my plan about having Thanksgiving on my turf—Mom had the opportunity to minimize my efforts. My festive tablecloth and coordinating napkins weren't enough.

"I can't wait to see how they turn out." I carried dishes to the table. With the aroma of seasoned turkey wafting through the kitchen, my stomach growled.

After a quick check to make sure the forks were on the correct side of the plate, I snuck back to the bedroom and called Haley. "Hey, how's it going?"

"Things are good. I mean, it isn't what I expected . . . at all."

"Did Hank invite Zach along?" I dropped onto the floor in the back of my closet and waited for an answer to a question Haley hadn't expected.

"Yeah, but it's not a big deal." Haley wasn't being straight with me, but there wasn't time now to prod her for an answer.

"Adam's parents and my parents are all here at the house. We're going to eat in just a minute, but everyone was busy with something, so I called to check on you."

"Go back to your company. I'll survive . . . probably."

"Have fun. Tell Zach I said sorry about his breakup."

She gasped. "I am not bringing that up. Then he'll know."

Another voice sounded from her end of the line, but it definitely wasn't Haley. It didn't sound like her brother either. "Then I'll know what, Carrot?" Zach must have been eavesdropping.

I laughed. "I'll talk to you later. Text me if you live through the night."

"Very funny." Haley didn't sound at all amused.

Adam glanced up as I walked back to the table. "There you are."

"Sorry I kept you waiting." I dropped into the chair next to Adam, trying not to laugh as everyone stared at the turkey napkin. Were we supposed to unfold them?

Mom pulled the pin out of hers then laid the colorful napkin that had been the feathers in her lap. "But you're good at keeping things, aren't you?"

I held my breath and drenched my mashed potatoes with gravy.

Adam's mom chimed in. "I guess you mean about how they dated without saying anything. Nearly broke my heart thinking he was cheating."

Adam pulled his bottom lip between his teeth. Hopefully his attempt not to laugh didn't result in a bloody lip.

"I was thinking of how they conveniently didn't tell us how she'd met Adam *before* the blind date." My mom passed the potatoes around the table.

My dad cleared his throat. "So were you just about to get into the bath or . . ."

Of all the conversations I never wanted to have at Thanksgiving, this ranked near the top of my list. But they'd brought it up. "In the bath. If it weren't for bubbles and leaves, I'd have—"

"That's enough." Mom put her hand up. "We don't want to hear anymore."

"I'm happy to tell the whole story. From how he was trying to hurry before all the bubbles popped to how he gave me a shirt and loaned me his fireman jacket. And, by the way, your bathroom towels are tiny."

Adam turned a deep shade of red. "Turkey turned out pretty good."

"It did." Mr. Cardona added more to his plate. "Thanks for making it."

Dad grinned. "Maybe y'all can host every year."

Both moms paled at the assumption included in dad's idea.

Adam gripped my hand under the table. "We'll have to see about that. Maybe just every other year."

Mrs. Cardona dropped her fork; my mom choked on her sip of wine.

Before either of them could ask any questions, Adam turned to his dad. "What time does the game start?"

That kicked off a conversation about football, and hosting Thanksgiving didn't come up again.

∽

Adam looked at me and pointed to the kitchen. "Want to help me get dessert?"

"Sure." I pushed away from the table.

He poked me in the side as we walked to the kitchen. "That was fun. Are you going to run away and hide again?"

"I wasn't hiding earlier. Haley is spending Thanksgiving with her brother, and I called to check on her." I served slices of pie while Adam poured cups of coffee. "I should get out the special doggie and kitty treats I bought."

"Where is Pookie? I haven't seen her in a while." He moved the cups and saucers to a tray.

Mom grabbed the creamer out of the fridge. "I let her out a bit ago. She was begging at the door."

"She's an indoor cat. She never goes outside." I bit my tongue, keeping back all the other words I wanted to say.

Adam pulled me close. "I'll go find her. Don't worry, okay?"

I nodded. "Did you let her out the front or back door?"

"The front. I'm sure she didn't want to share the back yard with those smelly dogs." Mom seemed unfazed by my mild panic attack.

Adam squeezed my arm before walking away. "Have dessert. I'll bring her home. Love you."

I pointed at the trays. "Mom, y'all enjoy. I'm going with Adam."

She blinked, her mouth hanging open.

"Did you hear me? Will you take this to the table?"

"He loves you?" Had she missed all the clues at dinner? Why was she just putting it together now?

"Yes. That's kind of old news, but yes. He loves me." I headed out the front door.

On his hands and knees, Adam looked under bushes, using his phone to shine a light into places the porch light didn't illuminate.

I looked under the cars. "Pookie! Here, kitty."

He walked to the gate and shined the light over the fence. Butch and Sundance barked with excitement. "Have you guys seen Pookie?"

"Why don't you call her, Adam? It's dark. She could be anywhere. How are we going to find her?"

He rubbed my arm. "Pookie, come here, sweet girl." Who wouldn't come when called like that?

A hesitant meow sounded in the branches of the big tree.

"She has a thing for trees, doesn't she?" He moved to the base of my large oak and pointed the flashlight into the branches. "Please come down. Don't make me get the ladder."

I grabbed his arm. "Should we call the fire department?"

"You're joking, right?"

The wind blew, and I shivered. "No. Isn't that what people do when cats get stuck in trees?"

"Have you ever seen a cat skeleton in a tree?" He reached into his back pocket. "Pookie, you can have the rest of the bag if you don't make me climb up after you."

She seemed excited about that idea. One branch at a time, she worked her way closer to the ground. But she was so little, and the tree was so big.

I covered my face, too nervous to watch. "Tell me when she's down."

"She's a cat."

"Just tell me."

He slipped his arms around my waist. "While Pookie makes her way down, we get a few minutes alone. You know what I'm most thankful for?"

"Are you trying to distract me?"

"Is it working?"

"Yes. What are you thankful for?"

"You. *And* Mr. Raymond."

I swatted his chest. "You're such a rule breaker."

"Maybe just a little." He rubbed his hands up and down my arms. "You cold?"

"Only a little. Oh, my mom heard you."

He flashed his lopsided grin, and those dimples appeared. "The love part?"

"Yeah, that. So, be prepared for questioning." Pookie jumped down, and I scooped her up. "You had me worried."

She wriggled and shoved on me until I set her down, then she sat at Adam's feet and meowed like a little angel.

He picked her up. "You can have the treats inside." He carried her into the living room and dumped the treats onto the ottoman. "Eat up before we let Butch and Sundance back in. They'll steal them from you."

Hand in hand, Adam and I walked back to the table.

His mom stood up. "When were you going to tell us that you were in love?"

Adam laughed. "I sort of figured it was obvious. I'm over here every chance I get, and I almost always have kitty treats in my pocket. But maybe I should've rented a billboard to broadcast the news."

Dad chuckled. "Seemed obvious to me."

Adam leaned in and kissed me. "I'm ready for pie."

If pie was code for something more, I was on board with that. "Me too."

CHAPTER 25

*G*litter was everywhere. Why did I choose this wrapping paper? Obviously, I chose the blue paper with the glittery snowflakes because it was stunningly pretty. I rolled out enough paper to cover the stainless-steel food trays I'd found for Adam.

For a guy who didn't like his food to touch, those would be the perfect gift.

Pookie ran onto the paper then flopped on her side.

"Get off. I'm trying to wrap."

Sundance trotted over, sure that he was missing out.

"Pookie, go play with Sundance." I picked her up and set her by her favorite playmate.

Butch stayed snuggled against my leg.

The last few times Adam went on shift, I'd been keeping the dogs. I liked having them around.

While Sundance kept Pookie entertained, I laid the trays in the center of the paper and folded the edges up, taping them into place. This was the last gift to be wrapped.

I was looking forward to Christmas more than I had in years past. I'd spent more on doggie toys and kitty toys than I should have, but watching them open gifts would be so much fun.

I grabbed the phone when it buzzed. "Hey, Haley. What's up?"

"Drop everything. I'll be there to pick you up in ten minutes."

"Why?"

"I need help shopping. Please." Haley rarely begged.

I stuck a bow to the top of the gift. "All right. I need to let the dogs out, and then I'll get my shoes on."

"Thanks. I owe you one." The call ended.

I tucked the gifts under the tree—except for the pet toys. Those went into the closet so they wouldn't get opened early.

I glanced down at my leggings and favorite t-shirt. Why bother changing? Adam was on duty, and I didn't care about impressing anyone at the mall.

After letting the dogs out for a potty break, I pulled on my shoes. "Be good, all of you."

Pookie licked her paws. She was too busy to listen.

"Butch, I'm leaving you in charge."

He was by far the most responsible.

Haley honked when she pulled up in front.

I blew the animals a kiss and locked the house before running out to the car. "So who are you shopping for?"

"My brother. He wants to get together for Christmas."

"Y'all going camping again?" I couldn't say it without laughing.

Grumbling, she rolled her eyes. "Maybe I can buy my brother a clue."

"What's with his sudden desire for family togetherness?" I hadn't seen her brother in a while, but from what I remembered, he'd never been all that interested in spending time with his little sister.

"He's been this way since he moved back home. I'm not

sure why, and he doesn't talk about it." She parked outside the mall. "Only happy talk now. It's Christmas. Let's start in the bookstore. I need to get something for me." Haley was practical that way.

∼

After hours of shopping, Haley pulled up to the curb in front of my house. "I'm not coming in. You don't mind, do you?"

"That's fine. I'll call you tomorrow." I carried my bags onto the porch and fumbled with my keys before unlocking the door. Once inside, I froze.

The dogs and Pookie weren't waiting at the door. A glass of wine and a small plate of chocolate truffles sat on the entry table. Next to them was a note that read: *A treat for you.*

"Adam?" I popped a chocolate in my mouth and picked up the glass of wine.

I couldn't imagine a different explanation, but where was his truck?

Following the trail of yellow rose petals and candles, I called out again, "Are you here? I thought you were at work."

The rose petals led into my bedroom. A votive candle in a small glass holder flickered from the floor just inside the partially open door. My heart went into full aerobic workout mode, and my pulse quickened.

I pushed open the door the rest of the way. The trail continued into my bathroom.

After sipping my wine, I followed the path.

The bathroom glowed with candlelight.

Wearing only a pair of gym shorts that had leaves taped to them, Adam dropped to one knee in the bathtub. "Eve Taylor, since meeting you, my life has been *bathed* in laughter. You rarely *leaf* my thoughts. I've *fallen* hard for you." He paused and flashed that grin I loved. "I hope you think this is funny. What I'm trying to say is that I love you with all my heart." He held out a small box with the lid open. "Will you marry me?"

I couldn't remember ever being so happy. Choked up with emotion, I just stood there, staring at the diamond solitaire.

"Eve?" He held out his hand.

I set the wine glass aside and clasped his hand. "Yes. A million times yes." I climbed into the tub with him. "And I think you're *treeeemendously* funny."

He slid the ring onto my finger then pulled the clip out of my hair. It fell around my shoulders, and his grin widened.

"You are beautiful." He tangled his fingers in my hair, and our lips met. For a few minutes, the rest of the world ceased to exist.

But then Pookie meowed from somewhere in the house.

"Oh no. She'll catch her fur on fire with the candles." I pulled away from Adam. "I need to go find her. Where are the dogs? I didn't eat all the chocolate."

He tugged me back to his chest. "She's crying because I locked her in a guest room. We'll rescue her later. The dogs are out back . . . far away from the chocolate."

"Okay." I melted back against him.

He dotted kisses on my neck then scooped me up.

"Whoa!" I clung to his neck. "You'll hurt yourself."

"I'll be fine. But thanks for that vote of confidence." He carried me down the hall. The candles had all been put out, and the house was dark.

As he stepped into the living room, the lights came on, and several people shouted, "Congratulations!"

Haley jumped up and down, clapping. "Yay!" She tossed confetti in the air. What a sneak.

Harper raised a glass then kissed Pookie, who was sitting on his shoulder. "Lookie who I found trapped in a bedroom."

Mom had tears running down her face, and rubbing her back, Dad narrowed his eyes when he saw how Adam was dressed.

Adam put me down and gave me a quick kiss. "I hope you don't mind a late-night celebration."

His mom ran up and hugged us both. "You look so happy."

Butch and Sundance darted into the living room as Adam's dad laughed. "I let them in. They wanted to be included."

I dropped to my knees and hugged both dogs. "Do you guys want to come live here?

Adam whispered loudly, "Say yes." Then he dropped down next to me. "I hope they didn't spill the surprise. I swore them to secrecy."

"They are as sneaky as you are." I cradled his face. "I love you."

He leaned in close so that only I could hear him. "And I love that you're wearing what you did on the day we first met."

"It's my favorite shirt."

"Javi wanted to be here, but—"

"Let me guess. He's visiting his girlfriend, isn't he?"

"Yeah. He's smitten. He drives up every weekend." Adam helped me up off the floor.

"Since you'll be moving out soon, maybe Javi should propose."

"Maybe so." He pointed to the kitchen. "Let's have dessert." As everyone walked that way, he tugged me back. "Soon is what I'd like too."

"Then you'll really get to see me in what I was wearing

when we first met." I trailed a finger down his cheek then hurried to the kitchen.

He kept pace with me. "Tomorrow? I'm free tomorrow." He winked and handed me a flute of champagne. "Care for some bubbly?"

"Yes, please."

Haley lifted her glass. "To my best friend and her bestest superhero."

Everyone but Harper raised a glass in the air. "A superhero. Really? Where do I find someone who will call me that?"

Adam laughed and pointed at our moms. "Maybe you should ask them to set you up on a blind date."

Harper shook his head. "I'm never going on another blind date."

"Never say never," everyone responded.

I'm not sure who said it first, but I'm pretty sure I said it the loudest.

EPILOGUE

HALEY

When it was time for the first dance, Adam held Eve's hand and led her out to the dance floor. She gripped his hand so tight, his fingers were almost white. Then they stopped in the middle of the dance floor.

Before the music started, he cupped her face with both hands and kissed her.

There wasn't a dry eye in the place after that.

The music started, and I dabbed my eyes, watching Eve's perfect wedding unfold exactly as planned. We'd spent so many hours thinking about every detail. And it was worth every minute.

Hair tickled the back of my neck. I wasn't used to wearing my curls wrestled up in a fancy twist. I brushed the errant hair away then went back to watching Adam and Eve. When the song ended, other couples made their way onto the dance floor.

Showing up single to weddings wasn't fun, but it had been my choice. Hopefully, Harper would ask me to dance. Otherwise, it would be a long reception.

The tickling started again. Had the air kicked on? It wasn't that warm. The February weather was perfect.

I turned to look for a vent.

"Hiya, Carrot." Zach grinned. "I wondered how long it would take you to turn around."

Dressed in a suit, he redefined good looking.

Butterflies started a rave in my stomach. "Hi. Why are you here?" I hadn't seen his name on the guest list.

"Eve invited me. I came to keep you company." He leaned forward and draped an arm around me as he pointed. "The guy over there—is that Harper?"

I nodded.

"Well, Harper keeps looking this way. If he asks me to dance, that would be awkward."

"What do you want, Zach?" Curt, I didn't know any other way to hide my feelings.

"Dance with me. Sitting here isn't much fun."

"All right."

He stood and held out his hand. "I promised Eve I wouldn't let you hide in the corner all night."

As soon as Eve returned from her honeymoon, she'd get an earful from me. I didn't need pity dances from my brother's best friend.

"Never mind." I crossed my arms. "I don't feel like dancing."

"Please. I'm not above begging." He grabbed the back of my chair and shifted as if he was about to kneel. Sometimes, he took his teasing too far.

"Do not make a scene." I popped up out of my chair. "I'll dance with you."

"Where is the happy couple spending their honeymoon?" He shrugged off his jacket and rolled up his sleeves.

I stared at his newly polished boots. "A cabin in an undisclosed location."

"Undisclosed, huh? You know where, don't you?" He pressed a warm hand to my back and led me onto the dance floor. "Which of us is going to lead?"

"I'll let you, I guess."

"I appreciate that." He leaned down to talk over the music. "You were saying that they're staying near here."

"I didn't say that. But they'll only be at the cabin two nights. Then they fly off to Mexico to enjoy a cabana near the beach." I tapped his chest. "Please don't tell anyone, Zach."

"Mum's the word. On a scale of one to ten how do you think Adam will rate as a husband? Will he be good for Eve?" Zach twirled me then pulled me back again.

"I'd say a twelve. He's perfect for her. I don't think there's *anything* he wouldn't do for her."

"Really?" Zach raised an eyebrow. "Anything? Would he really have given up his dogs?"

I stepped closer and kept my voice even. Thinking about how in love they were made it hard not to tear up. "In his heart, he knew she would never have asked that. She knew what was important to him. It's part of who he is."

The song ended, but Zach didn't let go. "What if he couldn't have both?"

I shrugged. The question didn't feel like it was about Adam anymore.

The music started again—a slow song—and Zach slipped his arm around my waist. "They look really happy."

I put my hand on his shoulder as we started to move around the dance floor. "They are. I've known Eve since the tenth grade. You were already away at A&M when she moved to town. I've never seen her this happy."

"What makes *you* happy?"

Somewhere deep inside, I think he already knew the answer. For all my attempts at subtlety, I failed miserably in that arena.

Before I could say anything—not that I had any clue what to say—Harper appeared next to us. "May I cut in?"

"I suppose." Zach let go of my hand. "Thank you for dancing with me, Carrot."

"Is he your chaperone tonight?" Harper always went for the laugh.

"Something like that." I was a mess. Dancing with a strikingly handsome firefighter, all I could think about was the guy who was off-limits and not interested.

"Do you know where they are headed after the reception?"

"I think Zach is headed home, but you can ask him." I could play dumb when needed.

"Funny. I meant Adam. My buddies and I planned a little surprise. We just need to know where to go."

I shook my head. "Nope." The song ended, and I stepped away. "Wait, did you put Zach up to asking?"

"I only asked Zach if I could cut in. I'm not sure he likes me." He winked. "I'm off to beg the info from someone else." Harper wouldn't have any luck. "Can I come find you again?"

"To dance, yes." Only three people knew where the cabin was, and I wasn't talking.

I found a corner and watched Adam twirl and dip Eve. Cameras flashed. The happiness etched on their faces would forever be captured.

When the deejay asked for everyone except the single ladies to clear the dance floor, I stayed put. There would be plenty of others ready and willing to dive for the bouquet of yellow roses.

Hidden in the shadows, I figured I was safe even when Eve scanned the room. But when she made eye contact with Zach and he walked over to the deejay, I knew I was about to be royally embarrassed.

Before the deejay could call me out by name, I marched out to the middle of the floor and waved.

That earned me a few laughs.

Beaming, Eve turned around and launched the bouquet into the air. Instead of diving for the flowers, the group of ladies divided like the Red Sea, leaving me to catch the bouquet or get whapped in the head.

I scanned the room, wanting to see Zach's reaction, but he wasn't anywhere to be found. How had he disappeared so quickly?

Embarrassed, I held up the flowers when people cheered then hurried to my seat.

The guys lined up to catch the garter. Based on the shoving, they seemed more eager to capture the prize than the ladies had been. When Adam threw the lacy, blue garter, the guys dove for it and tackled each other in an effort to claim victory.

One of Adam's friends, a guy named Javi, stood and held up his hand, the garter hanging off his finger.

I brushed away another tickle on the back of my neck. "Why didn't you go out there?"

"Poor Harper. He tried really hard."

I crossed my arms and didn't bother to turn around. "Be nice. He's a really sweet guy. If I had any sense, I'd have come as his date."

Zach leaned around to look me in the face. "You turned him down?"

I nodded, avoiding his gaze.

He pointed across the room. "They're getting ready to go. We should see them off."

I wasn't about to miss the big send-off, but this was the hardest part. Reining in my emotions, I jumped up. "I need to be out there."

Zach grabbed my hand and steered me through the crowd. He picked up sparklers on the way out. The crowd gathered outside.

He pushed his way through, getting me to the far edge. Zach positioned himself across from me, and we held out our sparklers, creating the final glowing arch.

Ducking down, Adam and Eve ran through, but she stopped in front of me. Zach slipped the sparkler out of my hand just before she hugged me.

"I'm so happy for you. Tonight was perfect." I brushed happy tears off her cheeks. "Absolutely perfect."

She pressed in close. "Too bad Zach didn't catch the garter."

"It wouldn't matter because I'd never date him."

Eve patted my cheek. "Never say never." Still beaming, she kissed Adam then gathered her dress and climbed into the back of the limousine.

The door closed, and they drove off into the night.

I waved until the taillights were no longer visible.

Zach stepped up behind me. "You may not realize it, but we're the last ones out here."

"Okay."

"What did she say to you?"

"Stuff that best friends say."

"Well, don't look so glum. She'll be back in a week."

"I know, but it'll be different." I turned to face him. "And glum? Really?"

"Care to dance a bit more?" He held out his hand.

"Because you promised Eve?"

His gaze dropped to the ground. "Why else?"

"Why not?"

Surprised, he looked up and smiled. "Good."

I slipped my hand into his and walked with him onto the dance floor. A few dances wouldn't hurt anything.

∼

Want to read more about Adam and Eve?
Subscribe to get a **BONUS epilogue**.
It involves an early morning bubble bath one year later.
www.RemiCarrington.com/subscribe/

A NOTE TO READERS

Thank you for reading! I hope Adam and Eve made you laugh a little . . . or a lot.

One Guy I'd Never Date, Haley's story, will be out soon, and you just might fall in love with Zach alongside her.

Be sure to check out my website at www.RemiCarrington.com for information about upcoming releases and to see my other books.

ALSO BY REMI CARRINGTON

Bluebonnets & Billionaires

Dating the Billionaire's Granddaughter
Next Door to the Billionaire
Charmed by the Billionaire
Second Chance with the Billionaire
Surprised by the Billionaire
Cheesy Romance with the Billionaire
Designed for the Billionaire
Road Trip with the Billionaire

BOOKS BY PAMELA HUMPHREY

Hill Country Secrets

Finding Claire

Finding Kate

Finding Treasure

The Chase

(a standalone spin-off with characters from the series)

∼

Cheesecake, Margaritas, & Candlelight

Just You

Just Me

Just Us

∼

Other Books

The Blue Rebozo

Researching Ramirez:

On the Trail of the Jesus Ramirez Family

ABOUT THE AUTHOR

Remi Carrington is a figment of Pamela Humphrey's imagination. She loves romance & chocolate, enjoys disappearing into a delicious book, and considers people-watching a sport. She was born in the pages of the novel *Just You* and then grew into an alter ego.

She writes sweet romance set in Texas. Her books are part of the Phrey Press imprint.

facebook.com/remiromance
twitter.com/phreypress
instagram.com/phreypress

Printed in Great Britain
by Amazon